HIGH VELOCITY

HIGH VELOCITY

THE SILENCER SERIES BOOK 8

MIKE RYAN

Cover Design by The Cover Collection

Edited by Graham Toseland

1

Recker and Haley had just made it to the large, glitzy hotel. The man they were looking for, Darren Harmon, wasn't that far ahead of them. They tried to head him off at the club he visited first, but they were just a hair too late. Harmon first popped up on their radar after texting a buddy that he was going out that night to some bars and clubs to find some women he could have his way with. He mentioned in the text he had something extra to help him in that regard, leading Jones to believe he was going to drug someone.

Jones found out Harmon booked a room at the hotel, though he didn't have enough time to find out the room number. It took him a little time to find out which bars Harmon liked to frequent. Since the information came in so late, the team didn't even have time to stake out Harmon's home address. When they got the alert from

Jones' program, they immediately started hitting bars and clubs in the area to try to find the suspect. Once Jones finally found the bar Harmon was likely to be at and when Recker and Haley arrived, they learned from the bartender Harmon had just left with a woman on his arm.

Upon arriving at the hotel, Recker and Haley showed Harmon's picture to a few people and asked if they'd seen the man, hoping they'd get lucky. Unfortunately, no one did. After asking around, Recker and Haley looked around the lobby, trying to figure out their next move.

Recker touched the com device in his ear to get in contact with Jones. "David, we're striking out here. You getting anything?"

Jones was feverishly typing away, trying desperately to come up with a room number. "I'm working on it."

"We don't have much time. It's not gonna take this guy too long to do what he came here for."

"I know. I'm just about there."

Haley then tapped Recker on the arm. "We might as well start walking the halls. It'll give us a head start. Maybe one of us will be nearby when he finally gets it. Or maybe one of us will hear something walking by."

Recker nodded. "If this girl's been drugged, we're not likely to hear anything. But it's a good idea, anyway. I'll do the even floors, you do the odd. Let me know if you find anything."

Recker let Jones know what they were doing as the two silencers broke up and started roaming the halls. The two men quickly walked down their respective floors, looking and listening for any potential signs of the man they were looking for. Even though they knew it was unlikely they were going to find anything, that was all they could do. They had to hope the woman would be able to scream, leading them to the room, or, if she had enough energy, run out of the room if the drugs hadn't taken full effect yet. But they still knew their best chance at finding them was Jones. It was a twenty-floor hotel with almost a thousand rooms. Without some type of fluke occurrence, Recker and Haley knew they were basically looking for a needle in a haystack.

As Recker walked through the first floor, Haley was done on the second at basically the same time. They each walked up their respective stairs to start searching the next floors.

"Chris, anything?"

"Negative."

They continued the pattern for a few more floors until Recker and Haley were on the fifth and sixth floors. By that point their hope was about to evaporate, even though they had a good chunk of the hotel still left. They knew there was nothing else they could do on their end. As they reached the end of their floors, Jones lifted their moods.

"Got it. Twelfth floor. Room 1226."

"On the way," Recker said.

Recker and Haley immediately raced up the stairs to get to the twelfth floor, though Haley was closer and would get there first. Upon getting to the twelfth floor, Haley threw open the door and ran down the hallway until he reached the room in question. He took a quick listen at the door but didn't hear anything. He had to take it on faith that Jones was right. If not, it would be quite embarrassing to walk in on someone who did not have ulterior motives at hand. He also didn't have time to wait for Recker, even though he wasn't too far behind.

Haley slowly jiggled the handle to see if they had the good fortune of it being unlocked, but they weren't that lucky. Haley took a few steps back and was about to kick it in before he remembered it wouldn't work. Jones had already told them the hotel doors were much stronger than residential doors due to having to meet a high fire rating, and being aligned with steel, it was likely security would be there long before Haley was able to kick it in. He took a few steps toward the door again and knocked loudly.

"Room service!"

Haley shook his head, figuring this had no chance of working. He figured he must have seen at least a hundred movies where something like this happened and he always thought it was ridiculous. It would never work. He knocked loudly again and looked down the hall to see if Recker was in sight yet. He wasn't. Haley put his fist on the door and was ready to pounce on it again. Before he could, though, the door swung open. The man on the inside seemed quite displeased he had to answer the door for something he didn't ask for.

"I didn't ask for any room service," the man angrily said.

Haley immediately recognized Harmon from his picture and pushed the door open further.

"What are you doing?!" Harmon asked, backing up.

Haley didn't bother to respond. Instead, he let his fists do the talking for him. He reached back, curled up his fist, and unleashed a right hand that struck Harmon's jaw, sending the stunned man down to his knees. With the man not being a threat for the moment, Haley took a quick look around the room and saw a woman on the bed who was only wearing a bra and underwear. She wasn't moving and at first glance appeared to be sleeping, though Haley suspected she was knocked out with the help of a drug.

Haley turned back around to face Harmon, who had gotten back to his feet, and now also had a weapon in his hand. Harmon had removed a pocket knife and was holding it in his right hand as he faced his intruder.

"I don't know who you are, but you made the wrong move coming in here," Harmon said, trying to sound tough.

Considering Haley was an inch or two taller and about twenty pounds heavier, he didn't feel much of a threat from the man. Seeing as how all he had was a small pocket knife, and Haley had a gun he hadn't pulled out yet, it was all the more unconcerning to him. Even without weapons, with all the hand-to-hand combat training he'd received over the years, there weren't many men Haley would feel uncomfortable facing.

"Is this the part where I'm supposed to wet myself?"

Haley asked. "Tremble in fear for what you might do to me?"

"You have no idea who you're messing with."

Haley smiled, seeing Recker standing in the doorway behind Harmon. "Well, considering there's two of us, I'd say you better stand down."

Harmon shook his head. "That's the oldest trick in the book. I'm not falling for that one."

Recker didn't say a word. He brought his gun out and took a good, hard blow to the back of Harmon's head with his weapon, knocking the suspect to the floor. Harmon was out cold. With the situation in hand, Recker took a step inside and closed the door behind him. He then stood over Harmon's body for a few seconds.

"Sometimes the oldest tricks are the best," Recker said.

"Girl's over here," Haley said, pointing to the bedroom.

"She all right?"

"Don't know. Didn't get a chance to check yet. Looks like she's knocked out. Either that or she's a heavy sleeper."

Recker knelt beside Harmon and checked his pulse. "He'll be all right in a few hours."

"Besides the lemon on his head."

"He's lucky that's all he got."

After kicking the knife to the other side of the room, Recker and Haley went into the bedroom to check on the woman on the bed. As they did, Recker let Jones know Harmon was subdued.

"David, we're in the room. Looks like we got here a little too late."

"Oh no," Jones said. "Is she dead?"

Haley stood next to the woman and checked her pulse. "She's alive. Gonna wake up with a headache though."

"Let's be thankful that's all she'll have."

"How you wanna do this?" Recker asked. "The woman's knocked out. Harmon's knocked out."

As they were talking, Haley started moving throughout the room, looking for some evidence. He was hoping Harmon didn't use his entire stash and that he still had more drugs out in the open somewhere.

"I'll call the police and tell them there's a disturbance in that room," Jones said.

"What good will that do?"

"They'll see an unconscious woman on the bed and do testing on her and hopefully discover some illegal substances in her system. I'll make sure I tell them I think the woman was taken against her will or something. Don't worry, she will be in the clear."

"This might help," Haley said, standing by the dresser and holding up a clear bag. It had a dozen small, round, white pills inside. Haley put his nose by the opening and took a whiff, but the pills had no odor.

"Hold on, looks like Chris might have found his stash," Recker said.

"Excellent," Jones replied. "I'll put the call in to the police now."

"What if she wakes up disoriented before they get here?"

"Can you tell how many pills she's taken?"

Recker looked over at Haley, who shook his head. "No, there's no telling how many were in here to begin with or how much is in her system," Haley said.

"Considering they didn't have that big of a head start on us and the fact she's already knocked out so quickly, I would say it's safe to assume she's got quite a bit in her."

"Then I'd say it's not likely she'll wake up before they arrive," Jones said. "The police should get there within five minutes."

"What about Harmon?" Haley asked.

"How incapacitated is he at the moment?"

"Very," Recker answered.

"Then leave him and get out of there."

"Roger that."

Recker and Haley looked at each other. "Time to hit the road?" Haley asked.

"I'd feel better if we tied this idiot up first."

Recker looked around but didn't have anything to bind Harmon's hands together. Recker did the next best thing and dragged his lifeless body over to the closet. Haley opened the door for him and Recker stuffed Harmon into the closet. Once they closed the door, they brought a chair over and nuzzled it just underneath the knob. It was unlikely Harmon would wake before the police arrived, but Recker wanted to be certain the criminal wouldn't make a surprise escape. With Harmon safely tucked away, Recker and Haley quickly left, scurrying out of the hotel before the police arrived. Just as Recker and Haley had gotten to their car, they noticed the police cruiser pulling into the parking lot.

"Looks like things are good here," Recker said.

After letting Jones know the police were there, Recker dropped Haley off at his apartment before going home for the night himself. They both came back into the office early the next morning since Jones said it looked like they were beginning to get a heavy workload with some new cases coming in. Recker was the last to get there, as usually seemed to be the case lately. It wasn't that he was late, as it was only eight o'clock, but the others didn't have a pretty girlfriend that prevented them from getting in earlier. But he usually made up for it by stopping for breakfast for the three of them.

As Recker made it into the office, though, he could tell right away something was going on. Haley was being still and silent, a telltale sign Jones was working on something and nobody wanted to disturb or distract him. Jones was sitting at his computer, flailing away at the keyboard at an unusually fast rate. Unusual in how he worked in an everyday manner. It was quite normal for him to act that way when there was something important and urgent going on.

"Should I ask?" Recker said.

Haley looked at him, his hand covering half his face. "You shouldn't."

"Well, he did say we had a heavy workload coming up this week."

"No, this is not that," Jones said.

"Oh. He is here," Recker said with a fake smile.

Recker put the bag of breakfast sandwiches down on the table as he maneuvered his way behind Jones to see if he could tell what he was working on.

"You know I don't like you sneaking up behind me when I'm trying to ascertain something," Jones said.

"Well, I'm sorry, professor, but you know you would make things easier on us all if you just came out and told us what the issue was."

Jones stopped typing for a second and turned his head to look at Recker as he made his way to a chair next to him. "There's been a killing."

Recker didn't sound impressed. "There's always a killing."

"Two of them to be precise."

Recker looked at Haley, still not seeming concerned about the matter. "OK. Would you now like to tell us what makes these two killings so important?"

"They're people we know."

The look on Recker's face turned more serious. Now he was concerned. He knew it wasn't Mia since he'd just left her at the apartment and she wasn't going in to work today. He quickly ran through the list of all the other people he knew, though there was one name that quickly jumped into his mind. "Tyrell?"

Jones stopped typing again to look at him, though this time he had a quizzical look on his face. "No. Why would you think such a thing?"

"Uh, because he's the closest person I know, and you haven't told me anything else. How about you ending our misery and telling us who's dead?"

"Oh," Jones said, almost seeming unaware he was keeping them in suspense. "Well it's two members of Vincent's crew."

A look of relief swept across Recker's face. "Is that all? You shouldn't do that, you know."

"Is that all? That's all the emotions you can muster?"

"Uh," Recker said, looking over to Haley for guidance, though none was coming. He then shrugged. "Sorry?"

"Do you not see the significance of this?"

Recker looked up to the ceiling, hoping the answer would somehow fall to him. "Uh, nope, I guess not. What's the significance?"

"The significance is the undisputed mob boss of this city, a man you know, a man we've worked with and have a business relationship with, has lost two members of his team."

"And?" Recker said, seeming very unconcerned. "To be honest, I'm still kind of ticked off at him for that whole police thing he got us involved with, so excuse me if I'm not exactly shedding a tear for him in this trying time."

"Regardless of that, you don't just go around killing members of his squad without expecting some kind of blowback," Jones said.

"And you think what? It's gonna come back on us? He's gonna think I did it?"

"Perhaps."

"Won't happen."

"Or that we'll know something about it."

"Doubt it."

"Or that he might expand on our business arrangement and try to get us involved in his business," Jones said, fearful of getting into a larger conflict they had no business of being involved in.

"That could be possible."

"Even if none of that's the case, that still brings up a bigger issue," Haley said.

"I think I can anticipate what you are about to say, but go ahead anyway," Jones said.

"Who's dumb enough to take out a couple of Vincent's men?"

"There's a couple more questions to add to that," Recker said.

"Which are?" Jones asked.

"Did someone take those guys out knowing they're Vincent's men? Or was it just dumb luck they didn't know what they were getting themselves into?"

"I wouldn't call taking out Vincent's men any kind of luck," Haley said. "Bad luck, maybe."

"I have one more to question to add to that," Jones said.

"Which is?" Recker asked.

"Do we have a new player in town?"

Recker and Haley looked at each other, wondering if that was the case. "Heck of a way to state your arrival," Haley said.

"Can you think of a better one?" Recker said. "If you're gonna come in here and challenge Vincent and try to take a piece of the city away from him, you better do it in full force. And you better announce yourself and your intentions early. Cause if you come in here and try to dance around, he'll chew you up and spit you out."

"So, how we gonna find out? Or are we?"

"I think we'll know the answer to that if any more of Vincent's men drop in the next week," Jones said. "Or if he retaliates, assuming he knows who did it."

"Or we could put some ears on the street," Recker said.

"What do you have in mind?"

"Who's the best guy we know at that?"

"Tyrell."

"If something's going on, he'll find it."

2

Recker was already in the diner, waiting for Vincent to arrive. It was the first time Recker could remember actually beating Vincent to a meeting. It'd been two days since Jones learned of Vincent's men being killed and Recker could only imagine the crime boss was a little unnerved the last few days. Recker took the liberty of ordering a coffee and a bagel while he waited. As he dug into his food, his phone rang. It was Tyrell.

"How's it going?" Recker asked.

"Can't complain."

"How you making out with that assignment?"

"Not too good, man. Listen, from the people I've talked to, nobody knows anything about them guys getting knocked off."

"Don't know, or just too afraid to say something?"

"Nah, they don't know nothing," Tyrell said. "But there's a lot of theories floating around."

"Which are?"

"Most people think there's a new player in town."

"Why?"

"Has to be. Nobody's gonna knock off Vincent's crew unless you want a war. And the only way you're doing this is if you're fighting for territory."

"Maybe it was an accident or some guys who didn't know who they were," Recker said.

"No, those guys were ambushed, man. Whoever took them out knew full well what they were doing."

"All right, well keep your ears to the ground and let me know if you hear anything else, huh?"

"You got it."

Recker went back to his food as he contemplated what he'd just heard. If it was true there was another player in town fighting with Vincent, Recker wasn't sure if that was actually good or bad. On the plus side, maybe it was someone that could keep Vincent in check in case he roamed a little farther with his ideas and priorities. On the negative side, it was one more person Recker would have to worry about. And it was possible that whoever it was might not be as easy to deal with as Vincent. Recker had just finished his food when he looked through the window and noticed Vincent's entourage coming. The men took their usual positions outside, while a couple others cleared the inside to make sure there were no hostile people waiting for the boss. Those men took another table further down as Vincent and Malloy walked in. Malloy stood near the door as he usually did while Vincent sat down at Recker's table.

"Even got our usual table," Vincent said with a smile. He seemed rather upbeat for a man who'd just lost a couple of men.

"I almost wasn't sure what to do with myself. First time you weren't already here waiting for me."

"Yes, I'm sorry about that. Had a few other important matters to attend to first."

"Funeral arrangements, maybe?" Recker asked.

Vincent glared at him for a moment, the pleasant look on his face evaporating due to the subject matter.

"I assumed that's what we came to talk about," Recker said.

"Since you've brought it up, what have you heard?"

Recker shook his head. "Nothing."

Vincent gave him a cross-eyed look, thinking that surely couldn't be true. "Come now, Mike, with all the information you and David are able to glean from a stroke of the keyboard, I'm sure something must have come across your desks."

"Well, I hate to disappoint you, but that's exactly what I'm telling you. Didn't find out about it until David saw it on the news. Put some feelers out on the street that came back empty. I'm afraid I got nothing to tell you."

Vincent seemed content with the answer, taking Recker at his word. "It's of no matter. I will find out who it is and crush them."

"Do you have any leads?" Recker asked.

Vincent stirred his coffee as he debated how much information to share. In the end, he figured there was no use hiding anything. "We had a few, unfortunately none of them panned out."

"You think it's a new gang looking to take over?"

"I do."

"Why?"

"How much do you know?" Vincent asked.

"Not a whole lot. Just that two of your men were killed by some factory or something."

"Well they weren't just killed by a glancing bullet or some type of skirmish in a deal gone sour. My men were ambushed. There were entrance wounds in their chests and their backs."

"So, they were set up."

"They were lured there. Then executed."

"What were they there for to begin with?"

"We'd gotten a call from someone looking to sell some weapons," Vincent answered. "They went there to look over the merchandise."

"For your own purposes?"

Vincent smiled, unusually forthcoming in describing his business dealings. "No, I've got agreements with various factions up and down the east coast for redistributing weapons. I get a shipment then pass them along for a higher price."

"What about the guy that made the initial contact with you about this?"

"A small-time guy we've done business with before."

"Think it was him?"

"No, he's not someone who has higher aspirations,"

Vincent replied. "He's quite content in his current rank in the food chain."

"Then someone got to him."

"We've already questioned him. He doesn't know anything."

Recker knew there had to be more to it than that. "Well if he set up the meeting, and you think he wasn't involved, then it came from someone else he's done business with."

"Trust me, he's already been dealt with in a sufficient manner. He's given us everything he knows. He gave us a name and phone number of the man he was working with. We've checked both out. They came back empty. A fake name and a phone number that leads to nowhere."

"Even trails that wind up empty start with something. Maybe you took the wrong path."

"Perhaps so. But we've taken that avenue as far as we can go for the moment." Vincent reached into his pocket and pulled out what looked like a business card. He put it down on the table and slid it over to Recker. There was a name and number scribbled on the back of it.

"What's this?" Recker asked.

"The name and number of the man we used to facilitate this deal."

"And why are you giving it to me?"

"Maybe you could put your resources to work on it?" Vincent said. "I can promise you, I will make it worth your while if you can provide me with any further leads."

"I'm not looking for money."

"I know you're not. That's why I'm not offering it. But

I'm hoping the promise of further considerations in the future on my part will be enough to entice you."

Recker smiled. "Don't you still owe me for saving your life?"

"Do I? I thought that had been repaid by you escaping from that police car."

"Hmm. Forgot about that."

"Are we still keeping score?"

"Never was to begin with."

"I've lost count how many times we've done things for each other," Vincent said. "I'd prefer to think of it as continuing to strengthen our already strong business relationship."

"That's a very lawyer-ish, CEO way of looking at things."

"It fits, does it not?"

Recker couldn't dispute it. The moment he heard the news of Vincent's men being killed, he knew he'd somehow get roped into it. But he also couldn't deny Vincent had been a strong ally of theirs. The times they needed help, and there'd been more than a few, Vincent was always there to lend a hand or bail them out of trouble. Recker picked the card up and studied the name on it for a few seconds before putting it in his pocket.

"I can't guarantee anything," Recker said.

"Of course. I understand."

As Recker put the card away, he stared at Vincent for a few moments, wondering if he should bring up the last case they were involved with. He still wasn't happy about feeling like he was used for Vincent's gain. Part of him felt like he should let it go since it was over and done with. But part of him wanted Vincent to know he knew what he did. Recker didn't like feeling he was being played for a patsy. In the end, he chose to speak out. Even if doing so in some way damaged their relationship, Recker wasn't keen on keeping secrets, especially when it made him look like an idiot. At least that's how it seemed in his mind.

"I'll give this a look for you, under one condition."

"Name it," Vincent said, not yet realizing what was about to come.

"I want the truth about that police thing you got me involved with."

"The truth?"

"You played a lot of games with me on that one and I can't say I'm particularly pleased about it."

"Such as?"

"Such as telling me you knew nothing about what was going on when you really did," Recker said. "I got credit for killing someone taking down police officers when I didn't have a thing to do with it."

"You didn't?" Vincent asked, still not willing to admit any involvement. "Who did then?"

"You wanna hear what I think went down?"

"Sure. Why not?"

"I think you either heard about, or dealt with directly, a rogue faction of cops who were starting their own little organization that was moving in on your territory. But you couldn't go around killing police officers, could you?"

Vincent smiled, already knowing Recker had all the

pieces of the puzzle figured out. "I'm intrigued with what happens next."

"Now, I'm not sure whether that's because you just didn't want the heat of killing cops, or because you've got men in the department on your payroll and didn't want to risk them turning on you."

"I guess it doesn't really matter in either case, does it? All amounts to the same thing."

"Yeah, I guess so," Recker said. "So, to keep up your charade, you play it like nothing happened on your end. You get me involved, get me in touch with a detective that's in your pocket, all in the hopes of distancing yourself from everything."

"Sounds ingenious," Vincent said with a smile.

"Almost. So, what else happens? You find some sucker you could pin everything on, send Malloy over there to take care of him, and conveniently let me find him a hair too late. Evidence is planted in his room, he's dead, I get the credit, your competition's eliminated, a cop killer's gone, everything's tied off so neat in a tiny little bow."

"So, what's the problem?"

"The problem is I don't like being played for a fool."

Vincent nodded, understanding his position. In truth, if he was on the other side of the table, he probably wouldn't have liked it much himself. "So, what do you want from me? An apology?"

"Just an acknowledgment that everything I said is correct and how it went down. And that it won't happen again."

It didn't take Vincent long to think about the proposition. Especially now he was asking for Recker's help again. He knew admitting his involvement in the matter wouldn't somehow come back to him or be held against him. "I bet you're a real good card player too."

Recker smiled. "I don't play cards."

"Maybe you should. Could probably win a lot of money."

"If I was interested in that."

Vincent nodded again, finally willing to admit it. "Fine. You win. Everything you said is a hundred percent true and accurate. You nailed it. There's nothing I can or will deny. So, what do we do from here?"

Recker shook his head. "Nothing. I just want assurances from you it won't happen again. I don't like working in the dark."

"You've got it. You've also got my apologies. I give you my word it won't happen again."

"I would hope not. I would like to think our relationship wouldn't be severed by something so trivial."

"I cannot argue there." Vincent then pushed his coffee away from him and clasped his hands together. "I hope that's now been settled to your satisfaction."

"For the moment. I'll see what I can find out with this," Recker said, taking the card out of his pocket again and holding it in the air.

A devilish grin came over Vincent's face. "I'll anxiously be waiting."

Recker immediately went back to the office, where he found Jones and Haley hard at work, both banging away at their respective keyboards.

"Hey, look, you two almost look like the nerd twins."

Haley let out a laugh, while Jones kept plugging away, not even breaking stride. "Flattery will get you nowhere," the professor said.

"Takes a lot to insult you," Recker said.

Jones finally looked up at him and smiled. "Complaining?"

"No. Just stating facts."

"Now that we're done with the comedy improv; can we get down to business?"

"Everything's fine. Finally got a confession."

Jones scrunched his eyebrows together and contorted his face. "Over?"

"That whole police scandal he got us involved in."

Jones looked disappointed. "Are you still harping on that? I thought we agreed to put that to rest. It's done and over with."

Recker looked over at the wall and sighed. "Yeah, well, it wasn't for me."

"What good did it do?"

"Got me the answers I was looking for. Relax, David, everything's fine. He acknowledged his role in everything."

The look on Jones' face suddenly changed to a surprised one. "He did?"

Recker nodded. "Absolutely. I told him exactly what I thought and what I suspected him of and he came clean."

"To everything?"

"One hundred percent. As a matter of fact, he even offered an apology," Recker proudly stated.

"He did?"

"Gave me his word he would never do it again."

"Now there's a man who's looking for something," Haley said.

Jones sharply turned his head. "Such as?"

"Man like that doesn't go around apologizing for his actions, or even admitting them for that matter, unless there's something bigger at play. There's something else he wants for his admittance of guilt."

Recker pointed at his partner as if he had just gotten a prize for getting the correct answer to a puzzle. "You got it."

"He wants something?" Jones asked.

"That he does."

Jones' shoulders slumped, and he closed his eyes, getting a sinking feeling they were about to be dragged into something. "What is it?"

Recker reached into his pocket and grabbed the business card Vincent gave him. He held it in the air for a few seconds for everyone to see, then tossed it down on the desk. Jones picked it up off the desk and looked at it for a few moments.

"Should I ask what this is?" Jones said.

"You shouldn't," Recker answered. "But I'll tell you, anyway."

As he waited for the answer, Jones passed it to Haley. "I can hardly wait."

"The name and number of the guy Vincent used to facilitate a gun transaction."

"And that interests us how?"

"Because Vincent believes that guy holds the key to finding out who ambushed his men."

"And he'd like our help in finding out?" Haley said.

"You got it."

"Wonderful," Jones said.

"Hey, I told you we were gonna get roped into this."

"Doesn't mean you had to agree to it."

"Well, what if this is a new arrival of someone in town and we don't like them as much as Vincent?" Recker asked.

"Whatever happened to not helping known criminals?"

"I amended that policy."

"To what?"

"Unless it somehow helps us."

Jones rolled his eyes and turned back to his computer to start working again. Haley handed the card back to him. "I guess we better get started then."

"Never know, maybe this'll be fun."

3

_____

Recker and Mia were sitting down at the table having breakfast before they went their separate ways for the day. Mia was doing a double shift today and wouldn't have another opportunity to discuss with him what was burning in her mind for the last week. And she didn't want to keep thinking about it for a few more days before talking to him about it. Though she knew what his likely reply would be, she still held out a faint hope she could somehow convince him.

"So, does it look like you guys are going to be busy in the next few weeks?"

Recker stopped chewing his food for a second as he pondered the question, thinking it was a strange one to ask. He shrugged it off though as he finished chewing. "About average I guess. Tough to say sometimes. You know how it is, sometimes things pop up at the last minute."

"That's what I figured."

"Why do you ask?"

"Oh, I don't know," Mia said, flashing him one of her smiles. "Just asking."

Recker wasn't convinced though. He knew what that face meant. Behind that sweet, innocent, sexy looking smile of hers was a devious plot in her mind. He was just waiting for her to spill it. But after a few more minutes of silence and sensing that the other shoe was ready to drop, Recker couldn't hold back his curiosity any more.

"So, uh, did you have something in mind that you wanted?"

"For what?" Mia asked, pretending to be clueless.

Recker cleared his throat before continuing. "Well, it kind of sounded like you had, you know, something in mind when you asked that question."

"What question?"

"About how busy we were."

"Oh, that question."

Recker faked a smile of his own. "Yeah. That one."

"No, not particularly. What makes you think I had something in mind?"

"Umm, I dunno, maybe because you never really ask that since you know how quickly things can change."

"Oh, don't I?"

"No, you don't."

"Oh. Well, I guess I was just making conversation."

Recker finished his food then pushed his plate away. "No. You don't just make conversation like that about my work. You always have specific things in mind if you do inquire about it. So, I know it's not just making conversation. You don't do that. So, go ahead and spill it. What's on your mind?"

Mia wiggled her mouth around and scrunched her nose at him, not liking that he figured her out. "So, do you think you know me so well because of what you do or because we've been living together for a while now?"

Recker smiled. "Probably a bit of both."

Mia grinned at him again, not knowing exactly how to say what was on her mind. She was almost sure he'd rebuff everything she'd say, anyway. But she held out hope if she phrased it just right, that maybe, just maybe, he might consider it. "So, um, you know, I was thinking..."

Recker thought it was funny how she was stumbling over her words and having trouble getting started. He figured it wasn't too serious or else she would have just come out and say it. "Thinking's usually a good start."

The comment drew one of Mia's playful stares. "Funny."

Recker laughed. "Just come out with it. Whatever's on your mind, just say it."

"OK. Well you know I have some vacation time coming up I need to use."

"Yeah?"

"Well, I was thinking about using some of it soon."

Recker shrugged, still not seeing what she was getting at. "OK. Yeah, sounds like a good idea. You could use the time off."

Mia smiled again, thinking it was cute how he was a world-class CIA operator and could track down any criminal he set out to get, but he couldn't figure out what she was hinting at. "Well, I was kind of hoping to get away somewhere. You know, like get out of the area for a week, actually go somewhere, like a beach or something. Some place like that."

"Oh," Recker said, not sure how he felt about it. He was a little surprised she wanted to go away by herself, but he didn't want to stand in her way either if she felt she needed some alone time.

Mia could see by the look in his face that he didn't exactly approve of the idea. "What? What is it?"

"Nothing."

"Yes, it's something. I can tell. I can always tell."

"Well, I don't want to sound like a jealous, obsessive boyfriend or anything."

Mia scrunched her eyebrows together, having no idea where his line of thinking was going. "But?"

"No but," Recker said. "You should if that's what you want."

"What I want?"

"Yeah. I mean, I'd obviously miss you and wouldn't want to be away from you, but if you feel you need to go away for a week or so, then I think it's a good idea and you should."

Mia closed her eyes and sighed. She put her hand up to her face and rubbed her forehead, thinking this was not how she pictured it going in her mind when she initially thought of this conversation.

"Uh, no, no, you don't understand. I wasn't planning on going by myself."

"Oh?" Recker asked, thinking he'd seen this scene play out in several movies. It was usually right about now the bombshell was dropped on an unsuspecting partner, having to pick up the pieces after being dumped for someone else. Mia could see in his eyes he was starting to have questions, other things going through his mind.

"No, no, nothing like that," she quickly reassured him. "I love you. I would never dream of doing something like that."

A sense of relief lifted off Recker's shoulders. "Then what are you saying?"

"I'm trying to say I want to go on vacation... with you. Us. You and me."

"Us?"

"Yeah."

"Oh." Recker turned his head away slightly and looked toward the floor.

That wasn't quite the response Mia had counted on. It wasn't even an objection. "What? What does that mean?"

"What's what mean?" Recker said, turning his head back to her.

"Oh. You said 'oh.' What does that mean?"

Recker shrugged. "I don't know. Just an oh."

"You don't just say oh."

"I don't?"

Mia shook her head. "No."

"Oh."

They stayed silent for a minute as Mia waited for a response. But as Recker's eyes danced around the room, she wasn't sure if he was thinking about it or not. She even suspected he might have even forgotten the question.

"Mike?"

"Hmm?"

"What do you think?"

"About what?" Recker asked.

At this point, Mia wasn't sure if he was actually being this absent minded or if he was purposely trying to avoid answering the question. It wouldn't have been the first time he completely tried to push a subject to the side he didn't want to talk about. It was sometimes his way of trying to let someone down easy, by not talking about whatever the subject was.

Mia then laughed, believing that's exactly what he was doing. "No, you're not gonna play that game with me this time."

"What? What game?"

"The avoid answering a question game, then talk about something else in the hopes I'll eventually move on to something else. That way you don't actually have to talk about what you don't wanna talk about."

Recker tried not to crack a smile. "Is that what I'm doing?"

Mia put her finger in the air. "That's exactly what you're doing and I'm not letting you get away with it. Not this time."

Recker shrugged. "OK."

"So, can we talk about what I said?"

"Which was?"

Mia rolled her eyes and took a deep breath. "The part where I asked about us going on vacation... together."

"Oh... that."

"Yes... that."

"I don't think I've ever been on a vacation," Recker said.

"That doesn't surprise me."

"I wouldn't know what to do?"

Mia looked at him in a disbelieving fashion. "You're not a robot, Mike. You just go somewhere, have a good time, relax, leave your worries behind, that's pretty much it. I think you can handle it. And, oh yeah... you don't have to shoot anybody."

"Not shoot anyone? That sounds depressing. Sure you're not sending me to some hospital or something?"

"Really?"

Recker laughed. "I dunno. Did you have some place specific in mind?"

"Not really. I just would really like for us to get away somewhere and have a romantic week together. Where we don't have to worry about hospitals, or guns, or cases, or work, or anything. Just the two of us. We could go to the shore or the mountains. Anywhere's really fine with me."

Even though Mia was excited by the proposition of them going away, she could tell her partner was not quite as enthused. He didn't have the same glow on his face as she did.

"Isn't that one of the reasons you guys brought Chris on?" Mia asked. "So he could take some of the pressure and responsibilities off you, so you had a little more time to relax. I mean, if you work every day, eventually you're gonna explode. Everyone needs some downtime. You gotta unwind every now and then."

"Yeah, I guess."

"What's the matter? Don't you wanna go somewhere with me?"

Recker gave her a face. "You know it's not that."

"Then, what is it? What are you hesitating about?"

"I don't know. I guess I hate change. Anything out of the routine makes me feel out of my element."

"I'm not asking you to go away forever," Mia said. "Just for a week. And it doesn't even have to be right now. Maybe in a few weeks, next month, the month after. I would just like to know we have something together that's outside of all this."

Recker got up and walked around the table. He took Mia's hand as he brought her up to her feet and put his arms around her. "We do have something outside all this."

Mia couldn't help but look somewhat disappointed, figuring her vacation idea was never going to happen. Recker gently caressed her chin, then tilted her head up so she'd look at him. He then kissed her lips and scooped her up in his arms, her legs straddling around his midsection and crossing together around his back.

"I'll talk to David about it," Recker said, finally getting a smile across his girlfriend's face.

"Promise?"

"I promise."

Recker then walked into the living room, Mia still

glued to his arms. He reached into his pocket and pulled out his phone.

"What are you doing?" Mia asked.

Recker gave her a flirty stare and smile. "Telling him I'm gonna be late."

4

Recker sauntered into the office, ready to get down to work after taking some extra time with Mia. He drew a crooked look from Jones as he did.

"So glad you could make it and join us this morning," Jones sarcastically said, eyeing him up and down.

"Well, I know how much you struggle to keep things together without me being here, so I figured I owed it to you and the team to show up."

Though Recker was smiling after his quip, Jones simply rolled his eyes, not wanting to admit he found it humorous. "Well, you look... refreshed."

"Oh, don't start this again."

A wry smile came across Jones' face as he turned back to his computer, figuring he wouldn't tease his partner too much this time. Sensing their bantering was done, Recker looked around the office and wondered where Haley was.

"Where's Chris?"

"While you were home in bed getting your groove on, we had something come up," Jones said, still not able to resist jabbing at him again. "He's out taking care of it right now."

"Anything serious?"

"Nothing too bad."

"Should I roll on it as backup?" Recker asked.

"I do not believe that will be necessary. It's a simple robbery attempt. One or two guys max. Chris should be able to handle it relatively easily. Neither guy has an extensive criminal history or are particularly violent."

"Newbies, huh?"

"I suppose one could say that," Jones replied. "Besides, you have something else you need to deal with."

"I do?"

Jones wrote some things down on a piece of paper, copying them from the screen, then turned and handed it to Recker. "Yes, you do."

"What's this?" Recker asked as he read it.

"What does it look like? A name and an address."

"But for what?"

"I have tracked down the man Vincent's supplier dealt with."

"Huh? Vincent said he'd already dealt with him and was convinced he knew nothing more about it."

"Yes, the supplier," Jones said. "But his supplier gave him a name and phone number of someone who didn't exist, remember?"

"Yeah, Vincent said it was a dead end."

"Yes, for him, it was a dead end. For me, it was not."

"What'd you get?"

"Well I've traced that fake name and number to another fake name and number, which led to another fake name and another..."

"I kind of get the point," Recker said, not really wanting to listen to the same thing repeatedly.

"Oh, well, anyway, everything led me to that name and number there," Jones replied, pointing to the paper.

"Donald Little. What do you know about him?"

"From what I can gather, he's a rather shrewd businessman. And while I have not had the chance to delve too deep into his background, I can say he has several questionable things on his record. And I don't mean record as in criminal, of which he has none."

"He's just into some shady stuff."

"Precisely. But he does have some rather loose connections to several criminal organizations, as well as individuals with no organization ties, which leads me to believe he is someone who may play on the outskirts of the enterprises themselves."

"He's a guy who sets things up," Recker said. "But doesn't get his hands dirty himself."

"From the looks of it."

"So, what does this guy do for a living? On paper, anyway."

"Private consulting."

Recker couldn't help but laugh. "If that isn't cover for doing shady stuff and screaming you're involved in illegal stuff, then I don't know what is."

"Yes, well, the odds are good. But we won't know unless you pay him a visit and talk to him."

"And what if he doesn't feel like talking?"

"We both know you can be... persuasive."

"You think this guy is directly involved in this?" Recker asked.

"I don't know. I can't say he definitely knows the parameters of what's going on, but I think it's safe to assume he knows the players in the game."

"This his house or his office?"

"As far as I can make out, he doesn't have an office."

"This guy's as dirty as it gets. I don't even need to see anything else."

"Well if this is his home, does he have protection?"

"Tough to say," Jones answered. "I have not uncovered definitive proof in either direction as to whether that is the case. To err on the side of caution, I would suggest assuming there are one or two."

"When you want me to head out?"

"No time like the present."

Recker went to his cabinet and removed a couple of weapons for his chat with Little, expecting it wouldn't be quite so pleasant of a time. After grabbing his guns, he started to leave the office, walking past Jones. Just as Recker got to the door, his mind turned to Mia for some reason. He started thinking of what they had talked about that morning. He kept staring at the door, wondering if he should mention something to Jones.

Though Jones wasn't specifically watching what Recker was doing, he did notice he walked past his desk after grabbing his guns. Without saying another word or having any more questions, Jones assumed he was leaving. With not hearing the door close, Jones stopped working and turned around, observing Recker standing there. It appeared to him Recker was just looking at the door. Thinking it was strange, Jones watched him for a minute, wondering what he was up to. After a couple minutes, Jones couldn't take the suspense anymore.

"Is there something wrong with the door?"

"No, looks all right," Recker answered.

"Then why have you been staring at it for five minutes?"

"It hasn't been five minutes."

"OK. Let's call it three and a half. Are you OK?"

"Yeah, fine."

"Then why are you inspecting the door?"

"I'm not inspecting it," Recker replied. "Just thinking."

"Perhaps you would like to share?"

Recker sighed, not really wanting to come out with it, but also didn't want to keep it bottled up inside for a while. He figured it was best to just say it and get it over with. He turned around and walked back over to the desk. Jones studied his face and automatically knew what it entailed. While he didn't know the specifics, he knew that face. He'd seen it before. It was that face Recker had when Mia said something that was troubling him. Something he didn't want to think about but was now forced to. Jones didn't even wait for Recker to begin.

"So, what was it Mia said that is bothering you?"

Recker looked puzzled as he sat on the corner of the

desk. "What makes you think she said something that's bothering me?"

"Please, Mike, I've seen that look from you before. It's obviously not something work related. Whenever you have a problem with Mia, you get a particular kind of look on your face."

"I do?"

"It's unmistakable."

"I'm gonna have to work on that."

"I'm quite certain whatever you do won't have the desired effect that you are looking for," Jones said.

"Thanks for the vote of confidence."

Jones smiled, but then turned his attention back to the issue at hand. "Anyway, enough kidding around, what is it you are having a problem with."

Recker rubbed the back of his head as he thought of how best to say it. "Mia sprung something on me this morning."

Jones' eyes almost bulged out of its sockets as he imagined what it could have been. He was already fearing the worst. "She's not, um, you know..."

Recker leaned in closer to him to try to figure out what he was trying to say. "What?"

"You know," Jones said, putting his hand on his stomach and making a circular motion.

Recker quickly denied the assumption. "Oh, no, no, no... no, nothing like that."

Jones looked relieved and wiped his forehead, even though there was no perspiration on it. "Thank heavens."

"Why would you even think such a thing?"

"Well, you were being somewhat secretive. Seemed like the thing to think."

"Oh," Recker said, then pretended to be offended. "What would be so bad about that?"

"Well, nothing..."

"What, you don't think I could be a father?"

"It's not that..."

"You think I'm not capable of having a child?"

"No, that's not what..."

"What, because we're not married yet?"

"Yet?" Jones said.

"You don't think I could handle a kid?"

"That's not..."

"You think I'd be a bad father?"

"No..."

"So, what is it?"

Jones figured there was nothing he could say at that moment that would satisfy him or end the conversation, so he thought it best to move on. Jones closed his eyes and scratched the side of his face as he collected himself. He tried to get their discussion back on track to what Recker's original problem was.

Jones clasped his hands together. "Can we get back to what we were originally talking about?"

Recker stared at him for a few seconds. "Which was?"

Jones put his hand on his head, almost sorry he asked to begin with. "Something in regard to Mia."

"Oh. Yeah. So, we were talking this morning at breakfast..."

"Is this before or after your little escapade?"

"Can you just let me get back to telling my own story without interrupting with questions pertaining to my love life?"

Jones couldn't help but chuckle. "By all means. Proceed."

"And it was before."

"How enlightening."

"Anyway, Mia was talking about taking a... vacation."

"And she wants you to take some time off to go with her."

"How'd you know?" Recker asked. "Did she already call you or something?"

"No, Mike, she hasn't called. But it doesn't take a genius to figure that out."

"Oh."

"So, what was your reply?" Jones asked.

Recker threw his hands up. "I don't know, what was I supposed to say?"

"Did you say anything?"

"I just said I couldn't make any promises, and I'd talk to you about it."

"Oh, great, so now if you go back to her and say no, she's going to think I put the kibosh on it and she'll be mad at me for you not going."

"I said I'd talk to you about it," Recker said. "I didn't say it was up to you."

"Well that's basically what you're implying."

Recker sighed. "Yeah, I know."

"So, what is it that's bothering you about this? You don't want to go?"

"No, that's not it."

"You think if you go you will be escaping from here and running out on your responsibilities? Or is it you think if you go you will somehow be letting us down or we'll think less of you? Like you are not doing your job anymore."

Recker made an expression that indicated his friend hit the nail on the head. "Yeah, I guess that's probably it."

Jones immediately tried to quell his fears. "Mike, when you took this job, when we started this, I never said it had to be a twenty-four-hour a day, three hundred and sixty-five days a year job. Now, I know we haven't taken much time off in the last few years, but I don't think that's been out of necessity. I believe it's been more because our life mostly revolved around here. That is no longer the case. At least not for you."

Recker's shoulder slumped as he thought of his situation even more. "I guess part of it is I feel like I'm being pulled in two different directions. On the one hand, I love Mia, I wanna spend more time with her. I wanna be the man she sees and deserves."

"And the other hand?" Jones asked.

"Part of me gets pulled to here even if I don't need to be. I feel like if I'm not here at least ten hours a day that I'm shirking my duties."

"Mike, that's never been an issue. You have always put in your time."

"I guess I don't want to disappoint you guys. You especially."

"That's something you never have to worry about. This

operation we've got going on has far surpassed my expectations when I first had thoughts of it. And you're a big reason why."

"I guess maybe it's just that things are different now," Recker said. "Things have changed. Change is hard for me. It's never been something I've accepted very well. I've always struggled with it."

"Change is inevitable. In our professional lives, in our personal relationships, nothing ever stays the same. We are always in a constant state of flux. The world spins around and we have to try to adapt to whatever is thrown our way. You either accept it and change with it or you reject it and wither away and die. That's the decision we all face."

"You always have a way with words."

"I think you should go," Jones said. "Not right this minute, but when this thing with Vincent is settled, when things die down a little, maybe a few weeks or a month, I think you should take her and go away for a week."

"You really think so?"

"I do. I think it would be good for you. Clear your mind, rejuvenate a little. There's more to the world than this little office and those streets out there. It won't blow up because you leave for a week."

"I would hope not."

"And if there's one thing I know about women, which albeit is not much, is you have to make them feel wanted and important. Or someone else will."

Recker nodded, feeling like his mind was made up on the matter.

"Besides, that is one of the reasons we brought Chris on, to take some of the load off your shoulders. Right?"

"Well, yeah, but not so I could see the world and leave you two guys behind."

"Mike, it's for a week. You don't have to feel like you're abandoning anybody. It's really OK."

"Yeah, this time it's for a week," Recker replied. "But what about after this? What about a few months from now or next year when she wants to keep taking things further?"

Jones smiled, thinking his friend was completely over-thinking and reacting to this. "Such as?"

"This time it's a vacation. But next time might be wanting me to do something else, change jobs, move away, start a family, take things to another level."

"It's like I said about change, it's always happening. Emotions change, feelings change, what we think today might be different tomorrow. When I first asked you to get involved in this, nobody said it had to be forever. We were taking things one day at a time. We never said we had to do this until we're eighty and they're putting us in the ground. Even me, who knows, maybe one day I'll decide I'd like to try my hand at something else."

"You really believe that?"

"Who's to say? Maybe one day I won't get the same level of satisfaction or I'll feel differently about what we're doing. It could happen. But I'm willing to roll with the punches as they come. I think you need to be more willing to do the same."

Recker nodded, sliding off the desk and onto his feet.

"Good talk, Dad, thanks," he said, tapping Jones on the arm.

Jones shook his head, trying not to show even the slightest bit of a smile as he watched Recker walk out of the office. "My pleasure, son."

5

Recker had been sitting outside Donald Little's house for nearly an hour, as he usually did when staking out someone new for the first time. He'd seen a few people come in and out, none of whom looked to be of the friendly variety. There also didn't seem to be any great security detail either. Though Recker did notice a man at the top of the long circular driveway, it seemed as though anybody could go in. There wasn't a gate at the end of the property to keep anyone out. Little's house wouldn't be considered a mansion, but it was a large house with five bedrooms, four bathrooms, three-car garage, swimming pool, and all the extra amenities one would expect in a house like that.

After sitting a little while longer, Recker figured he'd seen all he needed to make a move. Watching the house for two hours gave him enough perspective to know how to handle the situation. He got out of his car and walked across the street to Little's property, walking up the long driveway. The guard, dressed in an expensive-looking suit, saw him coming but did nothing to stop his approach. Once Recker got relatively close, the man put his hand up to stop him from coming any closer.

"What kind of business you got here, bud?" the man asked.

"Oh, just wanted to talk to Little."

"Yeah, you and a bunch of other people. Nobody gets in without an appointment though."

"Oh, you need an appointment."

The man nodded. "Yep."

"Oh. Well how do I go about getting one of those?" Recker pleasantly asked.

"Let me put it this way. If you don't know, you ain't getting one."

"Oh, so it's like that, huh?"

"It's like that."

"I don't suppose if I slipped you a few bucks under the table you could amend that policy, could you?"

The man didn't reply, and instead, just stared at Recker with a menacing scowl on his face. That was all the answer Recker needed, not that he seriously expected his offer to work.

"No, I guess not," Recker said.

"Take a hike, man, and go through the proper channels."

"Well, how am I supposed to go through the proper channels if you won't tell me what they are?"

"Figure it out. If you don't know, you don't know the right people."

"And here I thought I knew pretty much everybody."

"Guess not," the man replied.

"Sure you won't change your mind?" Recker asked, getting ready to take matters into his own hands. "This is your last chance."

"Last chance for what?"

"To not have to go to the hospital."

The guard laughed, finding Recker more comical than an actual threat. He put his hand on Recker's shoulder and gave him a push to spur him on to leave the property. Recker immediately grabbed the man's wrist and twisted it around, causing the guard to moan as the pain radiated through his arm and shoulder. Recker then stepped under the twisted arm and delivered a hard kick to the man's gut. With the guard hunched over, Recker unleashed several overhand punches to the side of the man's head, causing him to fall over. Though the man was hurt, he wasn't yet incapacitated, which Recker needed to happen. Recker took out his gun and walloped the man over the back of his head, knocking him out cold. Recker felt the man's pulse, to make sure he wasn't more seriously hurt. Though he was sure the man probably wasn't on the proper side of the law, he didn't have any motive to kill him, yet.

Recker didn't want to leave the guard lying on the ground in full view of anyone who might be going by so he grabbed the man underneath his arms and dragged him over to the front door. He figured he could stash him inside once he got in. Recker rang the doorbell and patiently waited for someone to answer. He didn't even seem concerned he had a knocked-out guard lying next to him. It was almost like an afterthought.

Recker rang the doorbell two times as he waited for the door to open. Finally, it did. Another rougher-looking gentleman appeared, also dressed in a nice suite. He immediately saw the body of the other guard and got on high alert.

"What happened here?" the man asked, putting his hand on the front of his jacket. Recker assumed the man had a gun inside it and was ready to pull it if necessary.

"Oh, I dunno, man, I happened to be walking by and saw this man passed out in front of the driveway there," Recker said, pointing to the area the man used to be standing. "I figured I should bring him up to the house so whoever was here could take care of him."

"Oh. Thanks. Did you see anyone else near him?"

"No, man, didn't see a thing. It was just him. If you want, I'll give you a hand getting him inside."

"Thanks."

The guard removed his hand from his jacket, seemingly no longer feeling a threat from the stranger. He stepped outside and walked around the passed-out guard's body, ready to pick him up. Recker quietly moved in back of the man and withdrew his weapon again. And once again, he batted the back of the man's head with his gun. The man immediately slumped to the ground, partially on top of the first guard. Recker also checked his pulse and was satisfied with his work thus far. He was two for two.

With the door open, Recker quickly took a peek inside the house. With no one else coming, he looked back to the fallen guards, wondering if he should drag them in or leave them where they were lying. They were on a small covered porch, hardly noticeable from the street, if at all, leaving Recker to figure they were OK staying where they were. Recker then went inside the house and locked the door, wanting to make sure nobody else came in. If the men woke up, he didn't want to be surprised by them. By locking them out, he assumed he would hear them making a ruckus to get back in the house or if they improvised trying to get in somewhere else.

Recker hadn't been in the house for more than thirty seconds before he saw another man approaching him. By the man's appearance, and considering he was dressed like the others, Recker assumed he was another guard. The man seemed to make a beeline for Recker.

"Can I help you?" the man asked, seeming like he was a little taken aback at seeing the stranger's presence.

"No, I'm good."

As soon as Recker uttered the words, he uncorked a right hand that landed flush on the man's nose, stunning him and knocking him back against the wall. With the man glued to the wall, Recker took advantage of his position and kneed him in the stomach, then delivered a few more punches to the man's face. Then Recker took the back of his head and repeatedly threw it against the wall behind them, creating a hole in the wall as a remembrance of the activity. Somewhere amongst the head bashings, the man passed out and slipped out of Recker's grasp, sliding down to the ground. With the man out of commission, Recker took a look around, hoping that was the last of the guards.

"Hope there aren't too many more of these," Recker whispered to himself.

Recker quietly walked through the hall and into a few rooms, finding the place eerily quiet. It was one of those times when it felt like somewhere along the way, someone was going to jump out on him and try to get the drop on him. It wouldn't have been the first time. But this was not going to be one of them. After he went through each room on the first floor, he found the house empty. He was starting to worry Little wasn't even there at the moment.

"Hope I didn't do all this for nothing," Recker said.

Recker walked through the kitchen until he came to a sliding glass door that led to a patio area. He stood there looking through it, seeing a man sitting at a round glass table, reading a newspaper. His back was to the door Recker was looking through. Recker, still feeling a bit uneasy thinking he may not have found the last of his trouble, took one last look around before heading out to join the man. Recker slid the door open and stepped outside, beginning to walk toward the seated man he assumed to be Little.

Once Recker got to the table, he stopped next to the man, pretending nothing was out of the ordinary. He saw some caviar on the table and helped himself to a spoonful. Never having the chance to have any before, Recker eagerly tried it, always wanting to see what it tasted like. Once the spoon left his mouth, he made an agonizing face as he licked his lips.

"What'd I tell you about eating that stuff?" Little asked, not bothering to look up at his visitor as he continued reading the paper. "You know, I was just reading about this guy…," Little said, suddenly looking up. The newspaper fell out of his hands as he jumped in his seat a little as he wondered who was standing next to him.

Recker still had a nasty look upon his face from the caviar. "Too salty."

"Who the hell are you?"

"How does anyone eat that stuff?" Recker asked, walking around the table and sitting down across from his host. "I mean, do you actually like that?"

"It's an acquired taste," Little answered, taking a look back to the house, wondering where his guards were.

"Oh, if you're looking for your goons, they're all taking a nap right now. They'll be fine in a little while except for the bumps on their heads."

"Who are you, and what do you want?"

"Just wanna have a nice little chat with you," Recker said, taking a look around. "Nice place you got here."

"Cost a fortune."

"I bet. You have maid service?"

"Of course."

"I figured you were the kind of guy who had people come in."

Little smiled, assuming the man had some type of business proposition to make to him. "Are we going to just talk about my comfortable lifestyle or are you going to tell me who you are and what you're doing here?"

"I'm getting to it."

"The suspense is killing me," Little said.

"Better hope that's the only thing killing you."

Little took a sip of his drink as he impatiently waited for his visitor to proceed. He looked up at the bright blue sky. "Sun only has a few hours left in it today. I certainly hope we have a resolution to whatever this is by then."

Recker smiled at him. He seemed cool and collected. Here was a stranger in his house and he didn't seem the least bit bothered by it. He had to know Recker was dangerous by now seeing as how he took out all the guards along the way. But Little wasn't rattled or nervous. Recker could tell this wasn't the man's first meeting in dangerous circumstances. He knew how to handle himself. Little was a middle-aged man, in his late thirties or early forties, but had a youthful appearance. Most people would have figured he was ten years younger than he actually was. He was of average height and weight with a full head of hair that looked like he just came out of a nineteen-eighties television show. He didn't have a particularly gruff appearance, and most wouldn't have assumed him to be in this line of work. But it usually served to his advantage as he stayed out of the limelight as was his preference. He didn't seek attention but loved the money and lifestyle the business afforded him.

"Let's talk about Vincent," Recker said.

"Who?"

"Maybe you've heard of him. Powerful mob boss,

connections everywhere, head of the major criminal element of this city. You recently sold guns to his enemies which helped kill several of his men."

Little put his hands up to dispute the facts. "Whoa, whoa, whoa, I haven't sold guns to anyone. And I don't know who this Vincent fellow you're talking about is."

Recker could appreciate the fact he wasn't willing to spill the beans just yet. He didn't figure Little would at first. He assumed he'd have to break the man down to get there. But Recker really didn't want to take too long to do it. Recker reached into his pocket and pulled out the paper with Vincent's contact and slid it across the table.

Little picked it up and read it. "Am I supposed to know this man too?"

"Yep. He's the guy Vincent had a deal with. He brought some people to Vincent with a weapons deal and the thing went sideways. Vincent's men were killed in the process."

"Don't know anything about that."

"Well, I think you do."

"Guess we have a fundamental difference of opinion then."

Recker looked unconcerned. "Guess we do. Maybe I should bring Vincent here to include him in this chat of ours. He might be interested in what's said."

Little's confident look slowly eroded. Up to now he assumed the man in front of him wasn't any kind of major player since he didn't recognize him. Recker took out his phone and scrolled through the numbers until he came to Vincent's. He slid his phone across the table, so Little could see he wasn't bluffing. He figured that once Little saw he really did know Vincent personally, maybe his tone would change, and he would be more receptive to answering questions.

Little looked at the phone without picking it up. "Am I supposed to call someone."

"No. Just pick it up. You might be interested in what's on it."

Little was a little hesitant to do so but did comply with the request. He picked the phone up and saw Vincent's name and phone number. He recognized the number. He also knew it wasn't something Vincent handed out readily. He knew if this man in front of him had it, he was a much bigger player in the game than he assumed him to be.

"So, who might you be?" Little asked.

"Let's just call me a concerned third party."

"If you want answers, then I need to know who I'm dealing with."

"I'm known on the street as The Silencer."

Little's face was now one of curiosity and caution. He obviously had heard of Recker's reputation as most in his line of work had.

"So, what role do you have in this turn of events?" Little asked.

"Vincent's lost a couple of his men. He wants to know who's responsible for it and he's run into dead ends. So, he's asked me to help him look into it."

"Interesting. I didn't know The Silencer got involved with those who fly under the respectability of the law."

"Vincent and I have helped each other over the years,"

Recker replied. "We have a respect for each other and basically avoid each other's interests."

"I see. So, what do you want with me?"

"My investigation has led me to you."

"I didn't have anything to do with that situation," Little said.

"I beg to differ. Now, you can either tell me and be done with it or I can call Vincent to include him in this little discussion we're having."

"He doesn't know you're here?"

"Not as of yet," Recker answered. "That can change rather quickly though."

Little stared at his visitor for a few moments as he considered his options. Though he really did not want to admit his role in anything, the last thing he wanted, or needed, was Vincent showing up at his house asking the same questions.

"So, what is it you would like to know?" Little asked.

"Just your role in what happened?"

Little sighed, not happy about coming clean. "If I admit to anything, I would like your word it doesn't leave this table."

Recker grinned. "Don't want it getting back to Vincent I take it."

"Something like that."

"As long as you weren't the one that killed his men, I don't think he needs to know every little detail," Recker said. "At least he won't hear it from me."

A slightly relieved look came over Little's face. "You must understand that I do business with Vincent. If he knows I'm also doing business with other people who might be looking to take him out that would look very bad upon me."

"Probably wouldn't do much for your future either."

"Yes, well, I guess you can understand my concern."

"I'm not interested in your business dealings other than the situation we're talking about," Recker said.

Little threw one of his arms up, resigned to the fact he might as well tell the truth. "Why not? As long as what I tell you stays between us."

Recker nodded, indicating it would.

"Very well. A group of men approached me several weeks ago about procuring weapons," Little said, remembering their initial meeting. "They said they were looking to start up operations around here."

"Did you know they were looking to challenge Vincent?"

"They didn't mention him by name, but it didn't take a genius to figure out what they were up to. I mean, if you wanna start making a name for yourself in this city, odds are you're going to be going up against Vincent at some point."

"So, how does that lead up to what happened with Vincent's men?"

"Well, I got them an initial shipment to start them out with. Everything went very smoothly. Then they started inquiring about Vincent and asked if I could set up a meeting."

"So, you did?"

"They paid me very handsomely to do so. Double my normal fee."

"And you didn't think that was strange?" Recker asked.

Little shrugged. "I am not paid to think. I am paid to facilitate transactions and bring parties together. That is all that concerns me. What happens with those parties after that is not of my concern."

"Well if all the parties wind up dead that will bring your little empire to a screeching halt, won't it?"

"Maybe, if they were the only warring parties in the universe," Little replied. "But we all know no matter what happens, no matter who dies, there will always be someone to replace them. Always. That's the way the world works. There will always be someone who is looking to take more... and do so in a forceful and violent manner."

"So, if what happens in these deals doesn't concern you then why did you use several fake names to make sure it didn't come back to you?"

"Because we both know Vincent's reputation."

"I think you're lying out your ass," Recker said. "You know what they were planning or else you wouldn't have bothered using other names. All you cared about was the money. I'm good with it. It don't bother me. Just say so."

Little sighed again. "Fine. I had a pretty good idea they were planning on using the meeting to ambush some of Vincent's men. I didn't really like it..."

"But the money was too good to pass up."

"Yes. OK? Is that what you wanted to hear?"

"Yeah, pretty much," Recker answered.

"If you wanna keep this out of Vincent's lap, then I need to know names, places, phone numbers, the works."

"You're asking me to betray a client's confidence," Little said.

"I don't care what you call it. You give me what I want, and I guarantee your name will never cross Vincent's ears. He is a rather big client of yours, is he not?"

"Yes. And if these other people find out I led them to you, what then?"

"They'll most likely be dead before they find out it was you and have a chance to seek revenge against you," Recker said.

Little was still apprehensive about handing over his information but knew he really didn't have other options. The man in front of him was in complete control of the situation. Little wasn't the violent type, that's why he employed guards, or else he would consider trying to take matters into his own hands. There was a small black bag sitting on the table which contained many of his secrets. He started to reach for it but was interrupted by Recker before he actually got to it.

"Before you pull anything out of that bag, I would hope you'd understand I'm probably a much better shot than you."

Little looked at him and gave him a wry smile. "It never even entered my mind."

"I know it didn't. You're much too smart to do something that stupid. I mean, why get yourself killed over something I could just take, anyway?"

"Exactly."

Little pulled the bag closer to him and unzipped it. He looked inside and saw his notebooks, a phone, and a gun. He took another glance at Recker, who by reputation, and by his own observations, didn't appear to be a man anyone wanted to mess with. Little bypassed the gun and gently removed the notebooks and phone so as not to make Recker nervous. Once they were plainly seen on the table, Little pushed the bag away. He started rooting through one of his books, getting to the page that had the information of the guys Recker was looking for. Little tore the page out, handed it to Recker, then closed his book. Recker eagerly read what was on the page. It was the name and phone numbers of three men.

"These it?" Recker asked.

"Those are the only three who I talked to."

"Do you know how many men are in this operation they got going on?"

"That, I couldn't say," Little answered. "They were understandably tight-lipped about their organization activities. And as far as my business was concerned, it wasn't on my need-to-know list."

"Are these three the top dogs or are they messenger boys?"

Little shrugged. "Who knows? They spoke like they had decision-making authority. They talked in a forceful manner. My impression was they were high up in the food chain. How high? Anyone's guess I suppose."

"Is this it?" Recker asked, holding the paper up.

"That's all I know. Don't know exactly who did the

killings, don't know anything about how this group operates."

"You have any other business with them lined up at the moment?"

"Haven't heard from them since that day."

"Possible they don't wanna lean on you and rely on you too much, knowing the relationship you have with Vincent. Might think you'll have second thoughts and turn them over to him."

"Possible," Little replied.

"All right, thanks." Recker pushed his chair away and stood up.

"I don't suppose you hire out, do you? I could use you in certain situations."

Recker smiled. "Not to the likes of you."

"Fair enough. I don't suppose we'll be seeing each other again."

"I dunno. Knowing what you do, I wouldn't bet against it. Oh, and uh, just in case this is a load of crap..."

"It's not."

"Well, a word of warning, if it is... you'll be seeing me again."

"I'm not worried about it." Recker started walking past the man, but Little sought further and final reassurance on their agreement. "Remember, not a word to Vincent as per our deal?"

"Not a word."

Little smiled as Recker walked back into the house, closing the sliding door behind him. Little went back to reading his newspaper as if nothing happened. He didn't seem the least bit concerned about Recker being in his house unsupervised. He assumed Recker would be leaving as quickly as possible before anyone else showed up. Recker didn't bother looking for anything else in the house. He had everything he needed. He didn't get the sense Little was lying to him or fed him bogus information. As Recker walked to the front door, he saw the man lying on the floor against the wall. He was starting to move around again. Recker wanted to leave something to remember him by and forcefully kicked him in the head, knocking him out again.

"Oh, sorry about that," Recker sarcastically said.

Recker then reached the front door and unlocked it, stepping outside onto the porch. Both men were still out cold. Recker stepped over them.

"You guys really need to stop laying down on the job."

6

_____

After visiting Little, Recker went straight back to the office. He wasn't about to tell Vincent anything yet until they'd thoroughly checked out the names on the list and knew what they were dealing with. Telling Vincent the names without them checking them first was a dangerous proposition he thought. When Recker got back to the office, Haley was back from his assignment and talking to Jones about it. They broke off their discussion when they saw Recker walk in.

"How was your conversation with Mr. Little?" Jones asked.

"Went about as well as it could go, I guess," Recker replied.

"What did you learn?"

Recker took the paper Little gave him out of his pocket and handed it to Jones. "I imagine this might help."

"What is this?"

"Names and numbers for the guys Little dealt with."

"Anything else?" Haley asked.

Recker shook his head. "No, that's all the information Little had. He said they weren't very willing to go into details on whatever enterprise they got going on."

"Stands to reason," Jones said. "Nevertheless, this should do nicely. It should at least give us a launching point."

"Let Vincent know yet?" Haley said.

"No, I don't figure he needs to know anything until we've got something worth sharing," Recker answered.

"Before I start working on these, should I ask if we're going to be in the news for anything?" Jones asked.

"Such as?"

"Oh, I don't know, dead bodies or anything?"

"What do you think I am, a haphazard violent person who goes around shooting everyone in my way?"

Jones looked at Recker and batted his eyes, thinking it was as loaded a question as he'd heard. He then looked at Haley, then around the room as he thought of how to answer. "I'm not sure I am the best person to answer that question."

Recker laughed, knowing he set one up on a tee for him. He was actually a little surprised Jones decided to strike out on the opportunity. "No, there are no dead bodies. Some injured ones, but not dead."

"He have guards?" Haley asked.

"Three. Not much of a problem, really."

As Recker and Haley talked about their latest assignments, going over strategy details, Jones started plugging the names into the computer. Gabriel Hernandez, James Milton, and Jamar Teasley. It didn't take long for the hits to come back on the computer. They all had lengthy and violent criminal histories, though none of them were originally from the Philadelphia area. Hernandez was from the Baltimore area, Milton from New York, and Teasley from Boston. There was no immediate connection on why they were now seemingly working together. And there was nothing in their pasts at this point to indicate they had crossed paths with Vincent at any time. As the team read their histories, they started throwing some theories around.

"Just because it's not obvious what the connection is to Vincent does not mean they don't have one," Jones said, cautioning them to not abandon that idea yet.

"It also doesn't mean they're the brains behind this operation either," Recker said. "Could be someone higher up the food chain who was aware of these three and brought them into the fold."

"Or it could be these three have a connection to each other and saw an opportunity here to take some territory for themselves," Haley said. "Start up their own gang with them at the top."

"Simply too soon to tell right now," Jones replied. "Any of the aforementioned scenarios could be realistically possible."

"How about we tap into their phone records and see exactly when they hit town?" Recker asked. "Then we can start piecing things together from there. Maybe see some common denominators. Work backwards."

"Sound idea. Why don't you guys go take a break for a couple of hours while I get started?"

"You trying to get rid of us?"

"Not at all. But you both have lives outside of here."

"I do?" Haley asked, not knowing what other life was being referred to.

"I think he's trying to give you a hint," Recker said.

"Oh."

"I'm not doing anything of the sort," Jones replied. "I'm just saying I don't need help with this and I can do it quite capably on my own. And probably faster."

"Well, I don't know about you, but I can take the hint," Recker said.

"Why don't you go have dinner with your better half or something? I'm sure she would love to see you."

"She's working a double."

"Maybe I should go out and get a girlfriend," Haley said.

"Please, no," Jones replied. "I'm not sure I can take both of you having a girlfriend at the same time. Do me a favor and wait a couple years first."

Recker and Haley laughed and joked around for a few more minutes before finally leaving the office and allowing Jones the solitude he was requesting. Haley decided to go home and relax for a couple hours, while Recker went straight to the hospital to see Mia. Though he knew she probably wouldn't be on break for another hour or two, he figured he'd wait, like old times before they actually got together. He went right to the cafeteria and found the table they used to always sit at as he waited.

As Recker sat down, he sent Mia a text message to let her know he was in the building. He didn't wait as long as he expected, as Mia's pretty face showed up only an hour later. She was surprised he was there but very happy to see him. She grabbed a few things to eat on a tray then joined him at the table, giving him a big hug and kiss.

"So, what do I owe this big surprise?" she asked, sitting next to him.

"Had some time to kill. Figured I'd spend it with the most beautiful girl I know."

A wide smile overtook Mia's face, happy to hear the sweet words. She leaned over and gave him another kiss, a little longer than the first one. "You sure know how to melt a girl's heart."

"Guess I've had a lot of practice."

Mia shot him a look causing Recker to start laughing. "You better not," she said.

"I'm just joking. I couldn't resist."

"Yeah, yeah." Mia started eating her food and couldn't help but think there was something else on his mind. Something important. "So, you gonna tell me the real reason you're here or are you gonna make me guess?"

"There's no other reason. Why do you think there is? Can't I just stop by and have dinner with you?"

"No, you can, and I love it when you do. It's just... not the normal."

"Well maybe we should make it normal."

"So, there's nothing else on your mind?"

Recker thought back to their earlier conversation at the apartment. "Well, maybe there is something."

"See, I knew it."

"No, nothing bad," Recker said. "I was thinking about what we were talking about earlier. You know, the vacation."

"Oh." Mia didn't sound very excited, mostly because she already had it in her mind they wouldn't go. She didn't want to get her hopes up only to have them dashed.

Recker could tell she thought she was about to get disappointed. "So, I already talked to David about it."

"Oh? And?" Mia asked, still not even the faintest bit of hope in her voice.

"He said he didn't see any problems with it."

"Really?" There was finally a hint of excitement heard in her voice, thinking they might actually have a shot at it.

"Yeah. So... I think maybe we should go."

Mia's face lit up and her eyes almost popped out of their sockets as she stared at her boyfriend. "Really?"

"Yeah."

"You really mean it?"

"Yeah, I think we should go," Recker said.

Mia lunged over and hugged Recker so hard he almost fell out of his seat. "Oh, I'm so happy."

Recker smiled, feeling good she was as happy as she was. She deserved to be, he thought. "You're sure you wanna take me on vacation?"

"There's nothing else I'd rather have."

"Not even a few diamonds or something?"

"Not even diamonds," Mia answered. "You're the only thing I want or need. I knew it from the moment I met you."

She planted another kiss on his lips as they embraced for a few more moments. After letting each other go, they went back to their respective seats and continued eating their food. They also started discussing vacation plans.

"So where should we go?" Mia excitedly asked. "The beach? The mountains? Somewhere warm?"

"Honestly, I don't care. It's up to you. As long as we're together and you're happy, that's all that matters to me."

"Well, I don't want it to be me making all the decisions. I want it to be the both of us."

"OK, OK. How about we talk about it over the next few days, then make a decision."

"OK. So, when can we go?"

"Well, we've got some things going on right now with Vincent, and possibly a new gang in town, so that might take some time. Let's wait a few weeks or maybe a month or so. Is that OK?"

Mia leaned in and put another kiss on his cheek. She was just so happy to hear him say he was going; she didn't even care about the date. "As long as we're going, any date is fine. I'll need about two weeks to put my notice for a vacation in here."

They continued to talk about their vacation plans for the rest of Mia's break period. Once it was over and she had to go back to work, all she wanted to do was throw herself into Recker's arms and go home with him. But since she had to work again, she settled for a hug and a kiss. As Recker left the hospital, he felt good he made Mia happy. She was really the only personal satisfaction he had outside of work. Nothing else mattered to him other than trying to make the city a safer place and trying to be the man that deserved her love.

Since Mia was working and he didn't have much else to do, and he didn't want to hang around at home, Recker went back to the office. He hoped Jones would have had, at least, something by now. It'd been about two hours. As Recker walked in, Jones was at his usual position, doing what he normally did. Working frantically between two computers, sliding his chair back and forth until he got the information he needed. Well, it always seemed a little frantic to Recker, but for Jones, who handled computers so easily, it really wasn't much effort as far as he was concerned. Recker sat down next to him and turned a computer on.

"Come up with anything yet?" Recker asked.

Jones turned his head and looked at him with a blank expression on his face. It was almost like Jones wasn't sure who he was. "How long have you been here?"

"Oh, about two hours."

Jones turned his head back to his computer as he stared at it, deep in thought it seemed. "Really?"

Recker scratched the back of his head, in disbelief of how absent-minded Jones could be at times. "Uh, no, not really. I just got back. Remember, you sent us away for a couple hours while you did your research?"

"Oh. Yes. Of course."

"You have no clue, do you?"

"Of course I do," Jones answered. "I remember perfectly. I'm not senile yet, you know."

"Good to know. So, do you have anything yet?"

"What would you classify as anything?"

Recker looked perplexed then put his hand up to his ear and started tapping it the way someone does after swimming when they're trying to get water out of his ear. "We must have a bad connection here or something."

Now it was Jones' turn to look confused. "What?"

Recker put his hand up, wanting to restart the entire conversation. "You know what? Let's just start over. Have you uncovered any other information about the three men you started digging into?"

"Oh. Yes. Why didn't you just come out and say so from the beginning?"

Recker rolled his eyes and looked at the ceiling, not even wanting to deal with it anymore. "So, what'd you find out?"

"First of all, Hernandez, Milton, and Teasley, have all been in other crime organizations, but none of them have ever been in charge of one, or even in the hierarchy of one."

"So, they're likely working for someone else."

"Correct. Furthermore, they all received and made calls to the same phone number in the week before Vincent's issue popped up."

"Someone brought them here," Recker said.

"Correct again. Now to this point, I have not yet pinpointed a name to go along with that number."

"Someone's trying hard to conceal their identity."

"Correct... again."

Jones went back to typing, leaving Recker alone with his thoughts. He sat there staring at the floor, rubbing his chin, thinking. Jones tried to ignore him and keep working, but he kept looking at his friend out of the corner of his eye. It always unnerved him when Recker was sitting there in thought, not doing anything. Almost as much as when Recker was out in the field looking to shoot people. Almost. Mostly because he knew when Recker got like that, in his thinking mode, he had a specific thought in mind that usually proved to be right. Finally, Jones couldn't take it anymore and stopped typing, swiveling his chair back around to face his partner.

"So, what are you thinking about?" Jones asked.

"Just getting things straight in my mind."

"Like what? What specifically is bothering you?"

"What makes you think something is bothering me?"

"Because I know that look."

"I'll have to learn to become less predictable," Recker said.

"Not likely."

"Yeah. Anyway, sounds to me like someone's building up an organization from the ground floor."

"For what purpose? To rival Vincent?"

Recker nodded. "Yeah. And it has to be someone high up, who's used to this type of thing, who has connections. Because these three guys are from three different areas. Only someone high up would know who they are and where to look."

"A mobster from another city, perhaps?"

Recker shook his head and continued thinking. "Not likely. Tough enough getting two factions to cooperate, let alone three." After another minute, Recker snapped his fingers, thinking he finally got it.

"What?" Jones asked.

"I think it's fair to say whoever's behind this isn't some run-of-the-mill thug, right?"

"I would assume so."

"I mean, this has involved planning, secrecy, involving other people while remaining in the background. That requires a certain level of sophistication."

"I would say as much."

"Someone who's done this type of stuff before," Recker said.

Jones shrugged, still not getting his point. "But all Vincent's enemies have been killed off, the other gangs destroyed, and any remnants still alive have been driven off long ago."

"Maybe we're not looking for an enemy."

"Well I certainly hope we're not looking for a friend," Jones replied. "With friends like that..."

"What if it's someone from another city who's retired, or was run off, or replaced, or relocated, something along those lines? They already know how to run organizations like this, they already know how to operate, and they know how to get things done."

"But for what purpose?"

"Maybe they see an opportunity. They see only one man in town and figure they can move in and take part of it. Or maybe they think they can take it all. If it's someone like I said, who was forced out somewhere, but still thinks they can be in charge, maybe they're looking at this as a new opportunity. They're aware of these other gangs and start recruiting from them, promising them higher positions, more money, more everything if they join him in this upstart group."

Jones took it all in, thinking it sounded plausible. Whether it was likely, he wasn't sure. But it was as good a theory as any of them had at that point. A few minutes later, Haley came back. Recker started talking to him about his latest idea and Haley bought in. While Jones continued running down the leads he had on the other three characters, Recker and Haley started researching displaced mob bosses who'd lost their power in the previous couple of years. As Recker started pulling things up on the screen, he sighed, thinking it was going to be more work than he thought it would be by the number of names he was seeing.

"This might take a while," Recker whispered.

Haley then tapped Recker on the arm. "Hey, I just had a thought that might make it a little easier."

"I'm all for that."

"What if we ask Vincent? I'm sure he would know far sooner and easier than we would. He's probably got all this information at his fingertips."

Jones couldn't help hear them talking and put his two cents into the conversation. "I would caution against that."

"Why?" Haley asked.

"Because we don't have proof of that being the case yet and we don't want Vincent going off half-cocked with information we don't yet have any validity of."

"David's probably right," Recker said. "Besides, if we

tell Vincent what we're thinking, he might go off on it alone and not tell us anything, thinking it's mob business."

"So? If they wanna duke it out, let them," Haley said.

"Problem is they might duke it out without it being the right move. And, in a situation like this, Vincent might try to cut the problem off head-on. I'm not sure that's the best move here."

"I would agree," Jones said. "I think our best course of action is working quietly, not letting those people know we're on to them and springing ourselves on them when they least expect it."

"Besides, we've built up goodwill with Vincent," Recker said. "I'd hate to throw it all away now for someone else."

7

Recker, Jones, and Haley had been working all night to try to figure out what they were dealing with. Since Mia was at work, Recker didn't have the inclination to go home and stare at the walls. It actually felt like old times, with him and Jones working all day and night, trying to get to the bottom of something. The three hadn't spoken in a while as they were all entranced in their own work and the room was deathly silent. The silence was broken when Recker's phone rang, startling them since they were not expecting a call. Recker grabbed his phone and looked at it.

"Who is it?" Jones asked.

"It's Tyrell."

"Wonder what he wants?"

"Maybe I'll answer it and find out," Recker sarcastically replied.

Jones rolled his eyes. "Indeed."

"Tyrell, what's up?"

"Yo, man, what's happening?"

"Nothing. Just working some things," Recker said.

"One of those things got to do with that Vincent mess?"

"Yeah, it would. Why? You got something?"

"Well you told me to keep my ears open, so that's what I've been doing."

"Whatcha got?" Recker asked.

"Ain't much, man, just a time and a place."

"Time and place for what?"

"I'm not even sure," Gibson answered. "All I know is something's supposed to go down at some abandoned building near center city."

"Center city's a big place."

"Well, yeah, I know, I got the address, it was just a figure of speech."

"Oh." Tyrell then gave Recker the address of the building. "So, what'd you learn?"

"Just that some deal's supposed to be going down there around ten o'clock tonight."

Recker looked at the time and saw it was just after eight. "Doesn't leave us much time."

"No, it don't."

"What kind of meeting?" Recker asked. "Who's involved?"

"That I can't tell you. All I know is it's some new group. Everything's very hush-hush. Might be those guys that hit Vincent last week. Can't say for sure but that's kind of the indication I was getting."

"Where'd you get this from?"

"Friend of a friend of a friend of a friend of a... girlfriend. Or something like that."

"Sounds reliable."

"Yeah, well, I didn't say it was. I'm just telling you what I hear. Up to you to figure out how reliable it is."

"What's your gut say?" Recker asked, trusting Tyrell's opinion, knowing he wouldn't intentionally pass on bad information.

Gibson paused for a second. "I dunno, man. Something doesn't feel right about it."

"Such as?"

"I dunno. I can't really put my finger on it."

"You don't think there's gonna be a meeting?"

"No, it's not that. I think there will be."

"Then what's the issue?" Recker asked.

"It's just... I don't know. I got a bad feeling about it for some reason."

"Well something's gotta be making you feel that way."

"Yeah, but I don't know what. Maybe it's just that it seemed like it came too easy. It almost feels like the information was supposed to get out and be passed on. Know what I mean?"

"I think I do."

"It almost feels like someone's being set up."

"I guess the next logical question would be who?"

"That I don't know, man."

"No ideas on who might be involved?" Recker asked.

"I mean, no, not really."

Recker then picked up a paper off the desk and started

reading the names. "Hey, did you ever hear of a Jamar Teasley, James Milton, or Gabriel Hernandez?"

"No, who they?"

"We think they might be involved in the Vincent thing."

"Oh. Well, no, I never heard of them before."

"All right, thanks. We'll check on the meeting."

"OK... wait a minute, hold up."

"What?"

"Now I'm thinking of it, I think I did hear one of those names before," Gibson said.

"Which one?"

"The first one you said. What was his name, Tease... Teasley?"

"Yeah, Jamar Teasley."

"When I heard about this meeting going down tonight. Someone said something about Tease is gonna handle it or something like that. I really didn't think nothing of it at first. Sounded like a nickname or something. Maybe they just shorted the guy's name or something."

"Yeah, could be. Thanks Tyrell, we'll check it out."

After getting off the phone, Recker immediately passed on the information to his colleagues, so they could start discussing its merits. They started checking other sources, looking on the computer, calling people on the phone, all in the hopes of somehow verifying the upcoming event. And they didn't have much time. Once Recker saw it was eight-thirty, he called off any further attempts to learn what was going on.

"All right, there's no use in going any farther with this thing," Recker said.

"What?" Jones asked.

"If this thing's going down at ten, it's already eight-thirty, we don't have time to keep going. We gotta move now."

Jones sighed, not liking the idea, but agreeing there wasn't much else they could do with such a short time frame. "I wish we had a few extra hours."

"But we don't. And we have to roll with the information we got."

"Do we? It's not necessarily something we have to do. We do not know for sure this is related to anything. In fact, it could turn out to be a complete waste of time. Or it could be something we don't even have to involve ourselves with."

"But, if it is?" Haley asked. "I don't think we can afford not to check it out. If it's a waste of time all we lose is an hour or two."

"I agree," Recker said. "We can't afford not to. Could be the big break we're looking for."

"And if it's a trap?" Jones asked.

"For who? It's not for us."

"One can never be too sure of anything in this line of work. You, above everyone, should know that. Everything is not what it appears."

"I'm well aware. I didn't say we should just roll in there in our tuxedos and plop ourselves down in the middle of the room and wait to be served. But if there's a remote chance this is somehow connected to Vincent's issue, then we need to check it out."

"It appears I'm being outvoted."

"We should probably get going if we're gonna scout the place out ahead of time," Haley said, mindful of the time.

"Yeah," Recker said, grabbing his weapons. "We'll call you with the details."

"I'll be anxiously awaiting your call," Jones replied.

Recker and Haley rushed out the door and into a car, traveling down to the abandoned building together. They got there with about half an hour to go before the meeting was supposed to take place. They drove by the building a couple of times to see if they could spot any activity going on or anyone else who happened to be waiting outside. They didn't notice anything out of the ordinary, however. Nothing other than it appeared to be an abandoned building. Judging by the heavy-duty equipment stationed all around it, along with the barriers that were set up everywhere, it looked like it was about to be demolished. It was a perfect spot for a meeting. Nobody around.

"Definitely looks like a good place," Haley said.

Recker drove around for a few minutes until he found a good place to park, eventually settling for a nearby parking lot. It was a couple blocks away and the pair quickly got to the abandoned building, trying to keep out of sight at the same time. They stuck to the sides of buildings, staying out of the light as much as possible. They snuck over a barrier in the back of the building, getting into the building through an opened window that had previously been knocked out. Once inside, Recker gave Jones a quick text letting him know they were there. After that, Recker and Haley worked up a plan. It was a large ten-story building they had to go through. They didn't know if anyone was there yet and they didn't know exactly where the meeting was supposed to take place. They wanted to clear the building first to make sure they weren't surprised by anyone already inside, but they also didn't want to be checking the building and have someone enter without them knowing.

"If we're both up there on different floors and someone comes through here without us knowing about it, we're gonna be on the outside looking in," Recker said.

Haley hesitated in replying, thinking about the situation before he offered up his own solution. "How about if one of us stays down here out of sight to keep an eye on anyone coming in? The other one checks the other floors."

Recker thought about it for a minute, eventually coming around to the idea, figuring it was probably their best option. "All right, who's gonna stay down here?"

"I'll take down here. If something comes up, I'll shoot you a message."

Recker nodded and took a deep breath before taking off, running through the first floor to look for the stairs. As he finally found them, Haley took another look out the window for visitors. After seeing the streets empty, he went around to check the other openings. Considering there were at least five or six doors, along with tons of windows, someone could have slipped in almost anywhere. Haley wouldn't be able to stay in one place and keep his eyes open on one spot. He'd have to keep moving around and checking them all. It was a tall task.

In only a few minutes, Recker was moving at a frenetic pace. He had already cleared both the second and third floors. With the building having seen better days, not all the walls were still standing, and most of the fixtures were no longer intact. But there were also no lights working, so it was tough to see in the dark. Recker thought about attaching a small flashlight to his gun to help him see better but decided not to use it as he didn't want to risk giving his position away by someone seeing the light before he got there. As he got to the fifth floor, Haley was starting to get anxious, wondering if they had company yet.

"How you making out up there?"

"No action yet," Recker answered. "Anything your end?"

"Quiet as can be."

"If this meeting's legit, we should be seeing something pretty soon."

Recker was more right than he knew. Almost immediately after saying the words, he thought he detected movement not too far from him. It sounded like someone stepping on some of the debris that littered the ground, mostly pieces of the walls and ceilings that had started crumbling down. Recker stopped dead in his tracks and listened for a minute, hoping to hear the sound again. And he did. He thought it sounded like too heavy of a step to be any kind of animal that would be up there on the fifth floor. He assumed birds, mice, or other smaller types of animals could have been up there, but none of them would have created heavy footsteps as they walked or scurried along. Only a person would have made the sounds he was hearing. As Recker listened, it sounded like the steps were moving away from him. He wasn't sure if he'd been made or if someone was doing the same thing he was doing, only doing it first.

Recker quickly moved in the direction he heard the footsteps moving to, hoping to catch up to whoever it was. Though he wanted to catch up to the person quickly, Recker didn't want to move so fast that he gave his own position away. He still tried to move as quietly as possible. He followed the sounds for several minutes until he reached the stairs. He let Haley know as he threw open the door.

"Chris, think I got someone up here. Going up to the sixth floor now."

Recker ran up the steps to the next floor, expecting to get a reply from his partner. He never did though. Now alarm bells were starting to sound in his head. There was no reason Haley wouldn't respond unless he had found himself in trouble. But if he was in a jam, Recker figured Haley would have let him know something came up. Or he assumed he would have heard shots. It was strange. Recker tried one more time.

"Chris, you there?"

Again, he got no reply. Now Recker had two choices. Continue after the man he heard or go back down to the first floor and check on Haley. In the end, Recker figured it was better to keep moving. Maybe it was just a bad connection preventing him from communicating with his partner. Or maybe Haley was seeing something but was trying to keep silent to keep himself hidden. And just maybe the man Recker was after could give him more answers than if he had gone back down to the first floor.

Recker threw open the door and slowly stepped out of the stairwell. Once he was completely inside, he was stunned and jolted to feel the cold steel of a gun pressed against the side of his neck. He closed his eyes, incredulous that he let himself walk right into it. His mind was preoccupied with what was happening with Haley that he didn't concentrate fully on his own actions.

"Turn around slowly," the voice told him.

Though Recker hadn't yet complied with the directive, he knew that voice. It was one he heard before. He slowly turned his head to the right as the gun was taken away from his head. While at first, his eyes gravitated toward the gun pointing at him, they eventually looked past it and at the man that was holding it. Recker was more than a little surprised at the face he was seeing. When he and Haley were en route to the building, Recker envisioned a lot of scenarios unfolding, but none of them included Jimmy Malloy holding a gun to his head.

"What the hell are you doing here?" Recker asked.

Malloy took his finger off the trigger of his gun and slowly brought it down to his side, eventually putting it back inside his jacket, letting Recker know he wasn't there for trouble. At least not with him. "Probably the same thing you are. Got wind of some type of meeting going down with possibly the people that hit us before. Boss sent me to investigate."

"Where'd you get wind of that?"

"On the street. One of our informants."

"What are you doing up here?" Recker asked.

"Didn't know where the meeting was taking place. Wanted to clear all the floors to make sure it wasn't going down up there. You?"

"Same thing."

"Hope it's not going on downstairs while we're up here."

"I got someone down there keeping a lookout."

Malloy smiled. "Ahh, the ever elusive partner we've been hearing about. Finally bringing him out of the shadows, are you?"

"Have to unleash him sometime, I guess, huh?"

They continued discussing what they knew of this meeting, wondering if either of them had heard anything different than the other. They hadn't though. In fact, they'd both heard the same story. Almost word for word. Not one different detail.

"Almost like someone wanted us to know," Recker said.

"Oh, you get that feeling too?"

Recker's head turned to look at their surroundings. "Got a bad feeling about this."

"Yeah, I hear ya," Malloy said. "You wanna soldier on and clear the rest of the floors together?"

"Yeah, I guess. I'm not sure we're gonna find anything to our liking though."

"Or maybe we just won't like what we find."

They took separate paths as they cleared the rest of the floor, Recker still trying to contact Haley. After determining the floor was empty of other visitors, Recker and Malloy spent the next few minutes clearing the rest of the floors. Once they finished up with the tenth floor, they stood in the middle of the room to discuss their options. Their next move was to descend to the main floor and figure out why Haley wasn't answering. If there was a crowd of people there, they'd have to be careful how they entered.

"Ready to go?" Recker asked.

"Let's do it."

Before they could enact their plan, though, the door to the stairs swung open, several men rushing through it. Gunfire erupted before Recker and Malloy even knew what was happening and could respond. Bullets were flying everywhere. Recker and Malloy dropped to the ground and removed their weapons to return fire.

"Looks like we got ambushed," Malloy said.

"Yeah, we were set up all right. Question is which one of us is the target?"

"Maybe both of us."

The sound of bullets ripping through the air and glancing off concrete was all that could be heard for several minutes as the battle ensued. Recker and Malloy were pinned down with what appeared to be five or six men attacking them.

"How we getting out of this one?" Malloy asked.

"Not sure yet," Recker replied, reloading his gun.

As the back and forth continued, no one appeared to be gaining the upper hand. Considering they were outnumbered, they thought it was strange their attackers weren't trying to get closer. They seemed to be content in how things were going.

"A little strange they're not being more aggressive, don't you think?" Malloy asked.

"Maybe they don't have to be."

"What do you mean?"

"I don't know. Maybe this is the plan," Recker answered. "Maybe they just wanna keep us busy for a while. Or maybe they got more people coming. Maybe they don't need to take any risks at the moment. Maybe they just figure on waiting us out."

"That's a lot of maybes."

"Sure is."

"I got one more," Malloy said.

"Yeah?"

"Maybe if we don't move soon, we're gonna get so up against it we're not gonna be able to get out."

Recker couldn't help let out a small laugh. "Maybe."

"So, what do you wanna do? Go out like gangbusters? Rush them?"

"Eh, I dunno."

Their plans were soon made for them as the door to the stairs swung open again. This time, it was Haley coming through it. He heard the ruckus and immediately rushed up the stairs. As soon as he came through, he got the jump on the other guys, immediately taking out three guys on his right. As he did, the three guys on his left jumped up and started firing at him. As they did, Recker and Haley saw their attackers making themselves visible, and the two men jumped up to fire at them as well. With everyone out in the open, bullets started flying in every direction. Men were dropping everywhere.

After taking out his initial three guys, Haley was shot by the others and immediately went down. Recker and Malloy unleashed their barrage at the three men, who had a little time to shoot back before they perished. Malloy also went down in the fray. Once the dust had settled, the only man left standing was Recker. He looked down at Malloy, who was holding his stomach and bleeding. He then rushed over to the men who had ambushed them to see if any of them were still alive. They were dead though. With not having to worry about anybody jumping up and shooting at him, Recker turned his attention to Haley.

"You all right?" Recker asked, looking at his wounds.

Haley coughed and smiled. "I've been better."

Recker looked at Haley's leg, which looked like it had several entrance wounds in it. He then put his hands on Haley's chest and arms, feeling for any other bullet holes. "You're not hit anywhere else?"

Haley laughed. "Isn't this enough for you?"

"Well, could be worse I suppose. You able to put pressure on it?"

Haley stuck his hand out for Recker to help pull him up. Once he got to his feet, Haley took a step, but the pain was unbearable, and his leg couldn't support his weight, causing him to crumple down to the ground again, though Recker caught him as he fell to cushion the blow.

"Looks like we got a problem," Haley said, trying to make light of the situation.

"Yeah, and you're not the only one."

"What do you mean?"

"Well I ran into Jimmy Malloy up here," Recker said. "Turns out he was here doing the same thing we were."

"Guess he knows about me now, huh?"

"That's the last thing I'm worried about right now." Recker turned his head to look in Malloy's direction, but he was still down on the ground, hardly moving. "He got hit too. I'm gonna go check on him."

"Go ahead. I won't move. I'll stay right here."

Recker smiled, then hurried over to Malloy's position. He could tell right away that his wounds were a little more serious than his partner's were. It looked like he was bleeding heavily from his midsection, but he was still alert as he held his stomach.

"Guess that was your partner saving the day?" Malloy asked.

"Yeah."

"Good deal."

"Yeah, well, not so good," Recker said.

"Why not?"

"Because now he's down too. All the bad guys are gone, but both of you have been shot, and looks like neither of you can move very well."

"Guess that is a predicament," Malloy said.

"And it's not my only one. Not only can I not carry

both of you at the same time, I don't know if there's any more of them down there waiting for us?"

"I've heard you can do just about anything."

Recker smiled. "Just a rumor."

"You tried calling for help?"

Recker pulled out his phone and dialed Jones' number, but it kept saying he had no service. Whoever it was must have been jamming the signal. He had a look of disgust on his face, giving Malloy all the answer he needed.

"Guess that's a no, huh?"

Recker let out a deep sigh as he looked around the room. "I'll figure something out."

8

————

Before doing anything about trying to escape, Recker's first order of business was to tend to the two wounded men. He tore some clothing off the dead men to use on Haley and Malloy to close off their wounds and try to prevent any more blood loss. Haley couldn't put pressure on his leg which meant he needed to be carried out. Recker didn't even want to attempt moving Malloy out of fear he might kill him by moving him. Recker went back over to Haley to brainstorm.

"So, what's the plan?" Haley asked.

"Don't have a good one yet."

"I suppose calling for help's no good?"

Recker shook his head. "Afraid not. Think they're using a cell jammer to block the signals."

"Figures. They sure set this up good."

"The way I figure it, we got two choices," Recker said,

not really liking any of them himself. "One, I leave both of you here until I can bring in the cavalry."

"Which is? We don't exactly have the police on our side you know."

"Probably Vincent. His guy's here too. He'd bring the rest of his crew and descend on this building like there's no tomorrow."

"And option two?"

"I put your arm around me and help carry you out of here as you're hopping on one leg."

"It'll take you forever to get out of here doing that," Haley said. "And if there's more down there waiting, it's not gonna be easy."

"I know it."

"What about Malloy under that scenario?"

"I'd have to come back for him. I can't carry two people out of here and he's too banged up to try."

"There's a third option," Haley said. "We all just stay here until help arrives. You know once Jones doesn't hear from us he's gonna get antsy. Once he tries to contact us and figures out he can't, he's gonna be worried."

"Who knows how long that'll be? The downside to that is we didn't come here loaded for bear. If they brought a lot more people to the fight, we're gonna be low on ammunition pretty quick. I don't know how long we'd be able to hold them off."

"So, what do you think the play is?"

Recker sighed and looked around the room. "I dunno. I don't really wanna leave you here."

"But it's probably the best move," Haley said, finally

saying what Recker wouldn't. "You'll move faster without someone weighing you down. Besides, I can stay here and protect him while you're gone. He'd be a sitting duck if we're both gone."

Recker reluctantly agreed and helped Haley get back to his feet, putting his arm around him so Haley didn't have to put pressure on his injured leg. Recker helped him hop over to Malloy's location, setting Haley back down beside him.

"So, you're the new guy, huh?" Malloy asked with a smile.

"So they tell me," Haley replied.

"At least we met with a bang."

Recker thought about leaving the two without much ammunition, then looked over at the dead men. He rushed over to them and pilfered their guns, as well as any ammunition he could find. He brought the weapons over to Haley, setting them down in front of him.

"It's not a lot but you're better off than you were," Recker said.

"It'll do."

Recker then looked at Malloy, who was in quite a bit of discomfort. "When were you supposed to check in with Vincent?"

"No set time. It'll probably be another hour before he starts getting fidgety if that's what you're thinking."

"Well, I'm gonna have to try to get a hold of him, anyway. I don't know how far they're jamming the signal for."

"Might not be that far," Haley said. "They jam it too far

away from this building, where other people are having problems, it might lead to complaints and someone looking into it. Probably something they don't want."

"Could be."

"If someone heard the shots, police might be on the way too."

"I kind of doubt it," Recker replied. "I think you'd be hearing sirens by now if they were. This isn't a residential neighborhood. It's late at night, business area that's mostly deserted, I don't think there's many people around to report it. Probably why they picked this spot."

"You should probably get going."

"Sure you'll be alright?"

"As sure as I can be."

"I'll be back as soon as I can."

Haley was positioned so he had a good angle to see the door, so he could see whoever was coming in. As he watched Recker leave, he hoped he wasn't seeing him for the last time.

"You know, if he gets shot or doesn't make it out of this building, we're as good as dead," Malloy said.

"Figured that was the case, anyway."

"So, how'd you get dragged into this thing, anyway?"

"I don't see how that's really a concern right now considering our predicament," Haley said.

"What difference does it make? You guys were former CIA, weren't you?"

"Even if we were I couldn't confirm it."

"I always had a feeling that was it. Either that or you were former military. Or even both."

"Hate to disappoint you, but we're not gonna sit here discussing my past."

"As mysterious as your friend," Malloy said with a cough.

"Just the way it is."

"So, did you know Recker from your previous life or did you get recruited blind?"

Haley kept his eyes and guns focused on the door, ready for another round of action. "Already told you, I'm not gonna talk about it."

Recker slowed down as he got to each level, almost expecting someone to jump out at him as he passed the door to each floor. As he passed a couple of floors, he worried about getting trapped. He envisioned a scenario where he passed a floor, only to have someone come out behind him, while at the same time, someone else jumping out from a floor he'd yet gotten to. That way they'd corner him in the stairway. He hurriedly ran down the steps hoping to avoid further conflict, even though he figured that was unlikely to happen. As soon as he passed the sixth floor level, the door swung open, revealing a figure in the doorway. Recker jumped back, startled, and immediately began firing. The man getting shot at instantly dropped to the ground, the bullets flying over his head as he covered up. Recker took a few more steps toward the man, a little puzzled he wasn't being shot at himself. When the bullets stopped coming at him, the man uncovered his head and looked at Recker.

"What the hell, man?" Tyrell asked. "You always shoot at your friends?"

A look of relief and horror came over Recker's face at the same time. He was relieved it wasn't an unfriendly person trying to kill him, but he was upset he almost killed his friend. He was a little quick on the trigger expecting someone else. Recker rushed over to him and helped him to his feet.

"What the hell are you doing here?" Recker asked.

"Well I thought I'd come over and give you a hand. Had I known you'd almost kill me I would've stayed snug in my bed."

Recker tapped him on the arm. "Sorry about that. I assumed you were someone else."

"Obviously," Tyrell replied, brushing himself off. "Who'd you think I was?"

"Well there's six dead bodies up on the tenth floor that tried to ambush us. I kind of assumed you were one of them."

"Well I'm not."

"So I see."

"Where's your partner? Leave him behind?"

"Kind of. He's still up there. Took a couple in the leg and had trouble walking," Recker answered. "Malloy's up there too. Took one in the stomach. He's bad and needs help soon or he won't make it."

"Man, that's rough. I had a feeling something wasn't right here. That's why I came over. The more I thought about it, it just didn't seem right to me. Thought I'd come here and give you a hand if you needed it."

"I could use all the help I can get right now. How'd you get in here? Anyone else downstairs?"

"Nah, man, I just came through a back window and started looking around."

"And you didn't see anyone else?"

"Only some mice."

"So that means there isn't anyone else or they let you come up so as not to tip me off."

With Tyrell now there, Recker hesitated for a minute before pushing on. Now there were two of them, he wondered if they should go back up and get the others. One could help Haley while the other helped Malloy. At least now he knew there was nobody else between the sixth and tenth floors. He knew he could get them at least that far without any further battles.

"If we go back and get them, Malloy might not make it if we're not careful," Recker said.

"Last I checked the elevator ain't working," Tyrell replied. "Even if Vincent's men come, it's gonna be awhile and they're gonna have to carry him down these same stairs, anyway."

"But at least they could try to get him out on a stretcher to minimize the damage."

"Six of one, half dozen of the other. When you get Vincent here, who's to say he won't bleed out? Which means all your planning goes to waste, anyway. And who knows, maybe we get out of here safely and they storm the building and take out Haley. Just my opinion, man, but I think you're taking a greater chance leaving them up there. But like I said, just my opinion. I'll go with whatever you decide."

Recker thought about it a few more seconds and

wound up coming to the same conclusion. He couldn't escape the nagging feeling something bad was going to happen to his partner and Vincent's right-hand man if he left the building with the two of them up on the tenth floor by themselves. Now with Tyrell there, he didn't have to leave one of them behind.

"Let's go get them," Recker said.

They rushed back up the steps until they came to the tenth floor. Recker slowly opened the door, knowing Haley was going to have a gun pointed at him.

"Chris, it's me," Recker said, hoping to avoid having to duck a bullet.

"Come on in."

Recker and Tyrell walked through the door, stepping over the dead bodies. Haley immediately noticed Tyrell walking behind Recker, surprised he was there. It was even more of a surprise Recker had returned so soon. Haley assumed that meant there was a bigger problem somewhere downstairs.

"Fancy meeting you here," Haley told Tyrell. "Welcome to the party."

"Well I didn't get an invitation, so I just figured I'd crash it."

"So, what's going on?"

"We're clear down to the sixth floor," Recker said. "So, we can at least get you to that point without a problem. Well, other than you guys moving around."

"I've been meaning to work on my hopping skills anyway," Haley replied.

"We don't know if there's anyone else here so keep

your gun available in case we get jumped somewhere along the line."

"Ready, willing, and able."

Recker and Tyrell then went over to Malloy. They both reached down and gently picked him up and got him to his feet.

"You gonna be able to make it?" Recker asked.

"Won't be winning any races but I'll make it," Malloy replied.

Tyrell helped Malloy walk over to the door, though very slowly, as Recker went over to Haley and put his arm around him. They hobbled out the door, making sure they didn't go too far ahead and leave Tyrell and Malloy behind without being able to protect them. Both injured men grimaced and groaned as they went down the steps, the pain radiating throughout their bodies.

"Just be ready as we pass by these floors in case somebody jumps out at us," Recker said.

"I hate surprises," Tyrell replied.

They continued moving slowly, taking a lot of time to go down the steps. After they got to each floor, they paused for a few seconds to give the injured men a little time to catch their breath. As they continued descending the steps, they were about halfway between the sixth and seventh floors when Recker suddenly stopped.

"What's wrong?" Haley asked.

"I heard something."

"What was it?"

"Sounded like someone walking up the steps," Recker said, looking over the railing as far down as he could see.

"Anything?"

"No."

"Sure you heard it?"

"Positive," Recker answered.

"Maybe it's friendly," Tyrell said.

"Only problem with that is the only friendly people we know are right here."

"Unless it's Jones or Vincent," Haley said.

"I think that's wishful thinking. Kind of soon for either of them to show up."

"What do you wanna do?"

"Keep going. No point in stopping now."

They passed the sixth floor without incident and stopped again once they got to the fifth. They had concerns about going any further.

"One thing's for sure, they gotta know we're here," Haley said. "Moving quietly, we're not. Not with me hopping all the way."

Recker knew he was right but wasn't sure how they could combat that. After a minute, he thought he'd come up with something. He had to hope that it would work.

"All right, if someone else is here, let's make them think we ducked out somewhere," Recker said.

"How we gonna make them think that?" Tyrell asked.

"By making a lot of noise."

Recker banged his gun against the metal railing so the clanging noise would be heard echoing down the stairwell several levels below them.

"Let's get in! Let's get in!" Recker shouted, making sure his voice was loud enough to be heard by anyone else.

Recker put his finger up to his mouth to make sure the others didn't say a word. He pointed back to the stairs they came from as he and Tyrell sat Haley and Malloy down, away from the door that led into the fifth floor. They stayed in position, almost paralyzed, waiting for someone else to come. They stayed silent as Recker stuck his head out, listening for the slightest of sounds to indicate someone was coming. A few seconds later he heard what sounded like footsteps shuffling up the stairs. He turned his head around to look at the others and stuck two fingers in the air to indicate two men were coming.

Recker then opened the door, making sure it hit the wall to give off another noise that could be heard. He wanted the men to have no questions about which door they ducked into. Recker then readied himself and stuck his gun out in front of him, ready to fire. He took a few steps back up the steps to give himself a higher vantage point once he saw the two men come into view. The sounds of the footsteps were growing louder and closer. Within a few seconds, it seemed as if the men approaching were almost on top of them. Recker tightened his grip on his gun, then loosened it as he relaxed his fingers.

A few seconds later the two men arrived, each holding a gun. Recker stayed back for a moment, silent and out of sight. He didn't recognize either of them. He knew they weren't Vincent's men. Recker was familiar with the faces of everyone in Vincent's organization, at least the ones Vincent didn't mind being identified. Vincent always figured it was best if Recker knew the names and faces of most of the men he employed, outside of his informants and contacts, that way, if Recker ever ran into one of them on a job, he would be less likely to kill them. One of the men slowly opened the door and took a peek inside, without going in yet. Recker stepped fully out into the stairway to greet them.

"Looking for me?" Recker asked.

The two men turned their heads and instantly swung around, guns pointed at him. Recker already had the drop on them though and beat them to the punch. He hit them with one shot each, then tagged them with another as they both dropped to the ground. Not sure if they were dead, Recker hurried down the steps and grabbed their guns. One of them was dead, but Recker could see the other was still breathing, though he wasn't moving very much. It didn't look like the man was very alert so Recker tapped his cheek a few times to wake him up more.

"Hey, who hired you?" Recker asked. "Why are you here?"

The man mustered up enough energy to spit some saliva out of his mouth. "Screw you."

Recker didn't take offense and didn't even get mad at the man's belligerence. He simply tapped his face a couple more times. "Who sent you? Who'd you come here for?"

"You're not getting out of this building, man."

Recker was starting to lose his patience, knowing he didn't have a lot of time to sit there and play games and dance around the truth. "Looks like you're bleeding pretty bad there. But it's possible you might be able to make it. I can give you two options. You can give me some answers and I'll leave you here breathing and maybe you can make it to a doctor in time. If continuing to live doesn't interest you, then I can put a few more bullets in you and put you out of your misery."

The man puffed out his lips, not believing anything he was hearing. "Don't be stupid. I'm not an idiot. We both know you're gonna kill me no matter what. You're not letting me leave here."

"Listen, I don't know you from a hole in the ground. I got nothing against you. Other than the fact you're here trying to kill me. But men like us, we should have some type of honesty amongst each other, don't you think? I give you my word."

The man took a deep breath, though it hurt to do so. He still wasn't sure he could believe Recker, but he figured he might as well choose the alternative where he at least had a shot at living.

"Who's the head man?" Recker asked.

"Don't know. All I know's who hired me."

"Who was that?"

"Guy named Hernandez."

"Gabriel Hernandez?"

The man nodded, trying to conserve his energy by not talking when he didn't have to.

"Why? What were you here to do?" Recker asked.

"They let word slip out on the street about some meeting here tonight. They wanted Vincent's crew to get word about it and come down here."

"So they could be ambushed?"

The man nodded again. "Yeah."

"How many men are here with you?"

"Uh, I dunno, about fifteen I think."

Recker immediately looked at Haley. "Eight more to go." Recker then turned his attention back to the injured man. "Where are the rest of the men waiting?"

"I'm not sure. Different spots."

"So why this play against Vincent?" Recker asked. "What do they want out of it?"

"Gabe said they were looking to take some territory off him. Let him know that a new power was in town."

"They wanna take him out completely?"

"Not sure. I don't know all the details. I'm not that high on the totem pole. I think they just wanna get their foot in the door to start with and go from there."

"And you don't know who's looking to take it over?"

"I've only dealt with Hernandez so far."

"Maybe he's the head guy."

The man shook his head. "No. He mentioned something about getting orders from someone. Never mentioned who though."

"Why aren't cell phones working?"

"They got a jammer down on the first floor."

Recker had all the information he needed. Staying any longer was risking someone else coming up on them before they were ready. "All right. Thanks."

"You gonna kill me now?"

"A deal's a deal. Hope you never come into my sights again though."

The man laughed. "Yeah. Me too."

Recker went back to Haley and put his arm around

him as they started descending the steps again. Tyrell was right behind them with Malloy. Suddenly, another shot rang out. Recker swiftly turned, ready to fire, assuming it was the injured man with a concealed weapon or something. But he was wrong. Malloy still had a gun in his hand, and as he passed the injured man's body, unloaded a couple of shots into him, finally finishing the man off. Though he was badly injured himself, Malloy was never out of a fight, even if he could barely walk. Recker locked eyes on him and gave him a puzzled look, wondering what he was doing. Malloy wasn't going to feel badly about it though, no matter what kind of looks Recker threw his way. Malloy had a different code of ethics.

"What? I didn't promise him anything," Malloy said. "Besides, he just tried to kill us. He don't deserve to leave this building alive. We'd wind up seeing him again. If not today, then tomorrow, or next month. I just made things easier for later."

Recker wasn't really pleased about Malloy shooting him, mostly because Recker gave the man his word. But he really couldn't dispute Malloy's logic about possibly seeing the man again if he left the building. There was a good chance of it. So, with that being said, and with other things more pressing, Recker wasn't going to harp on it. They kept moving. Once they got to the fourth floor, they stopped, expecting to run into some more company. They stayed still for a few minutes as they waited, but eventually moved on after nobody appeared.

"Maybe they're saving everyone for the main floor," Tyrell said. "Have one big, huge firefight."

"Maybe," Recker replied, thinking it was entirely possible.

Once they got to the third floor, they stopped again for a minute as they waited for another visitor. This time it proved to be the right decision. Recker and Haley stayed put as Tyrell moved ahead of them with Malloy.

"Using us as bait?" Malloy asked.

"Got a problem with it?" Recker said.

Malloy laughed, though he coughed at the same time. "No, not really. I'd probably do the same to you."

Once Tyrell and Malloy passed the door and started going down the steps, the door flew open. Two more men appeared in the doorway, guns in their hands as they took aim at Tyrell and Malloy. They didn't even take notice of Recker and Haley to the left of them, waiting higher up on the stairs. As the men showed themselves, Recker and Haley instantly fired on them before the men were able to do the same to their friends. Both intruders went down immediately with head shots, dead long before they even hit the ground. After hearing the shots, Tyrell and Malloy turned around to see the damage that had been done.

"Guess we should say thanks?" Malloy asked.

"Save it for when we get out of here," Recker answered.

Recker and Haley then took the lead again, doing the same waiting game on the second floor. There wasn't any activity this time. They waited a few more minutes before traveling down to the first floor. They stood just behind the door that opened up to the first floor.

"By my count there should be six left," Recker said.

"Assuming that guy was telling you the truth," Malloy replied.

"I got a feeling as soon as we open that door we're gonna be ducking," Haley said.

"Good possibility," Recker said.

Recker knew there was a good chance that as soon as the door opened, a barrage of bullets would be heading in their direction. With two men having a hard time moving, he wasn't sure they'd be able to maneuver out of the way in time. Then he figured out another plan.

"You guys stay out of the way and against the wall," Recker said.

"What are you gonna do?" Tyrell asked.

"Experiment."

"This ain't science class you know."

"If they're out there waiting for us, as we assume they are, there's no way we're all gonna get through that door without getting hit."

"So, what do you have in mind?" Malloy asked.

"You guys stay here. Cover my tail. If anyone comes down that stairway to sneak up behind me, you know what to do."

"You're gonna take out the rest of them?" Tyrell asked.

Recker smiled. "Why not? There's only six of them. The odds are in my favor."

Tyrell started laughing. "That's what I love about you, man, never a doubt in your mind who's coming out on top."

After putting Haley against the wall, Recker got down and swung the door wide open. As soon as it opened, several rounds of automatic gunfire were heard. All four men inside the stairwell ducked down as the bullets glanced off the walls around them. Recker started making his way to the door again when he was stopped by Haley grabbing his arm.

"I can go out there with you," Haley said.

"What are you gonna do?" Recker asked. "Hop over the bullets."

"I can still crawl. I'm not out of the fight."

Recker thought for a minute before realizing he could probably use the help. Crawling out the door was probably the only way they were making their way inside unscathed, anyway.

"All right. You take the left and I'll take the right," Recker said.

Recker and Haley got down on the ground and opened the door, hearing another round of gunfire headed for them. They crawled out the door, each of them going in a different direction. As the door closed behind them, Tyrell wondered if he'd wind up seeing them alive again.

"Think I should go out there and help them?"

"Tyrell, gunplay has never exactly been your specialty."

"Yeah, well, desperate times call for desperate measures. Isn't that how the saying goes?"

"If I were you I'd stay right here," Malloy said. "Besides, they're not expecting you out there. They might shoot you by accident."

Tyrell then thought back to earlier in the night when

Recker almost shot him coming out of the fifth floor door. "Yeah. You might be right about that."

It was dark inside the building, but there were pockets of light coming in through the windows, thanks to a bright full moon. Recker was crawling along the floor as quietly as possible, trying not to give his position away. He came across some small, broken pieces of concrete and took a handful of it. He then turned on his side and threw it across the room, hoping for a reaction from their opponents. He got the desired result. Upon hearing the noise of the concrete hitting the floor, the men opened fire at that spot, giving their position away. Recker then jumped to his knees and fired at what he could make out as faint outlines of the men's bodies. Within a few seconds, he heard the sounds of bodies violently thumping down on the ground.

As Recker hurriedly scurried along the floor to get out of the line of fire, since he blew his own cover, the men turned in his direction to fire. As they started firing, Haley crawled along the other side and had a few of them in his sights. With his wound, he wasn't as quick to get to his feet or knees, so he continued to lay on his stomach as he took aim. He fired several rounds at the outline of the men, getting the same result Recker did. Within a few seconds, they heard the bodies of two more men hitting the ground.

As Recker continued crawling, he suddenly saw the leg of a man in black pants almost directly beside his head. He knew he was in a lot of trouble and quickly turned over and fired up at the man, just as the other man fired at him. The bullets fired at Recker hit the ground in the spot he was before he rolled over. Recker's shots landed in the man's midsection, causing the man to fall on top of Recker. Another man came racing over to the shots and started shooting at Recker, though the bullets wound up lodging into the body of his dead friend that shielded Recker from the lead. Recker then aimed his gun up at the man, though it was hard to do so with the weight of a two-hundred-pound man on top of him. Suddenly, though, a few more shots rang out, and the man fell to his knees, blood pouring out the holes in his chest. That gave Recker a much easier target as he fired a few more rounds, finishing the man off. Once the man slumped to the ground, Recker looked past him and saw Haley slithering on the ground. They gave each other a salute as Recker got to his feet.

Recker took a quick look around and saw no one else hiding in the shadows. He then walked around the floor to make sure there was nobody else there. Once he knew they were alone, he went back to Haley and got him on his feet again. He then went to the stairway and knocked on the door to let them know it was him, that way nobody had an itchy trigger finger and shot him by accident. Once he got a confirmation, he opened the door.

"We're good to go," Recker said.

"Good thing you announced yourself," Tyrell said. "I was about to return the favor for that little incident you pulled upstairs."

"You'll have to wait for your revenge another time."

"I guess I can let it go this time."

"So, you guys wanna get out of here or are you starting to feel at home?" Recker asked.

"It is starting to grow on me a little."

"As much as I like the banter, you think we can do it after I get these slugs out of me?" Malloy asked.

"You wanna go to the hospital or does Vincent have a guy?"

"Just call Vincent. He'll set it up. Might as well take your guy there too."

Tyrell picked Vincent up and the four of them headed out of the building.

"You guys sure know how to party," Tyrell said.

"What do you mean?" Recker asked. "This was just a regular night for us."

9

Recker and Vincent were sitting in the waiting room as they waited for the doctor to come out. After leaving the abandoned building, Recker called Vincent and explained the situation. Vincent had him go to a doctor that was on his payroll. Tyrell helped get the wounded men there, then took off as soon as the doctor started checking them out. While they were waiting, Recker called Jones and explained everything that happened up to that point. Dr. Luke was a licensed doctor and had his own practice, but he also did some work off the books and behind closed doors for extra money. He was a very skilled doctor and had done work for Vincent's organization many times over the years. As long as the money was there, Dr. Luke could be trusted to keep whatever private work he was doing silent.

"Seems like a pretty good setup for an underground doctor," Recker said, looking around the room. "Not the usual stuff you'd find like no lighting and bars on the windows and things like that."

Vincent laughed. "That's because he's not some hack who happens to hatchet people up on the side. This is his work. He's a good doctor. We've used him many times over the years."

"Saves on your insurance deductibles I'm sure."

Vincent smiled. "Not really my main objective in coming here. Secrecy is a much more valuable commodity."

"So, what are you gonna do if you lose your right-hand man in there?" Recker asked.

"It's not something I have to worry about right now. Jimmy will pull through. Thank you for helping him through it. We're lucky you were there."

"Why did you only send him? Kind of dicey, don't you think?"

"At the time we thought stealth was the best option. Figured with a meeting like that, it was better to send one man. We weren't looking to get into a gunfight. Our only goal was getting as much information as possible."

"How'd that work out for you?"

"Well, we did get some information out of it. We know the meeting was a sham and there is a specific new threat trying to take over the city," Vincent said. "It must be someone with a high profile who has experience in these types of things."

"What makes you say that?"

"Only someone who knows what he's doing and done this type of stuff before would have the patience to sit back and wait, operate in the shadows. People who are new at this overstep their boundaries, they get too eager, make mistakes. They can't wait to project themselves and show everyone who they are. Can't wait to make a name for themselves. That's how I know this person, whoever he is, has power behind them."

"You're worried about him," Recker said. "I can tell."

"I worry about things I cannot see. That's why I need to get to the bottom of this quickly, so I can prepare countermeasures."

"Out of curiosity, would you be willing to concede control over certain parts of the city to prevent a large scale conflict?"

"You mean would I give up part of my territory and hand it over to whoever this person is? To avoid a war?"

"Yeah."

"An interesting question to ponder to be sure," Vincent replied. "One I couldn't possibly answer at this time. Not until all the particulars are known."

"Just a thought."

"Well since we're dealing in hypotheticals, I'm sure this isn't the scenario you had in mind for me meeting the new member of your squad."

Recker shrugged. "I knew it would happen at some point. I didn't have any preconceived ideas about how. With what we do, I figured it would probably be some time that wasn't very convenient."

After being in the doctor's care for a couple of hours, he finally came out of his little operating room, which was divided into a couple sections in case he had several patients. As he walked out, Recker and Vincent both rose from their chairs, anxious to hear the news about their friends.

"So, what's the prognosis?" Recker asked.

"Well, I'll start with your guy first," the doctor replied. "He's in relatively good shape. Bullet didn't hit any major organs or anything, just muscle tissue. He won't be able to walk around on his own yet, so he'll probably have to use some crutches for a week or two."

"And after that? Long ranging effects?"

"Will probably take around six weeks to heal, I would say. He'll still have to do some physical rehab for a while to get his strength back. Probably won't be able to run any marathons and walk uphill or things like that, but he should get back to almost where he was before. Might have some numbness occasionally, but if he does some rehab, shouldn't have too bad of a long-term issue."

"Good to know. Thanks."

"Just keep him out of firefights for a little while."

"Do my best."

Dr. Luke then turned his attention to Vincent. "As for Malloy, it looks like he'll pull through. The bleeding's stopped, he's stable, he'll have to stay here a few more days though so I can keep an eye on him, just in case."

"OK. Long-term prognosis?" Vincent asked.

"We're probably looking at a few months' worth of recovery time. He's not getting back in the saddle in a few weeks. It'll take some time."

"But he should get back to where he was?"

"In time, yes. But he can't push it too soon or he'll rip

everything open again. I know he's your go-to guy, but if you want him to get back to a hundred percent, he needs time."

"Well then, we'll have to give it to him." Vincent put his hand on Dr. Luke's arm. "Thank you, Doctor. You'll receive a payment in the next few days."

"No rush," Luke replied. "I know you're good for it. I better get back in there."

"When will they be able to leave?" Recker asked.

"Haley should be able to leave tomorrow. I want him to stay overnight for observation, make sure infection doesn't set in. As for Malloy, he'll have to stay a few days since his injury was a little more severe."

Dr. Luke then left the room to tend to his patients again, leaving Recker and Vincent alone.

"You gonna be able to survive a few months without your top guy by your side?" Recker asked.

Vincent smiled, realizing the question was somewhat tongue in cheek. "He's not the only member of my organization I trust or employ you know."

"But he does draw the top assignments. Especially with an emerging threat on your hands. You gonna be able to handle it?"

"Why such concern?" Vincent asked. "Are you throwing your hat in the ring to replace him? Finally taking my employment offer? If so, I might be able to arrange it."

"No, I think I'm still good."

"No need to worry about me. I'll make do with what I have."

Recker smiled. "I wasn't worried."

"Do you need a lift out of here?"

"No, Tyrell walked and took a bus after he left so I still have the car."

The two men parted company, with Recker going straight back to the office, where Jones was nervously waiting. Even though Recker had previously told him Haley's wound wasn't life threatening, Jones was still anxious to hear the results. Having any of them shot was an altering dynamic that would affect them all. Jones was waiting by the window when he saw Recker pull in then went to the door to let him inside.

"Not used to having a doorman," Recker said as he walked in.

"How's Chris?"

"He'll be fine. On crutches for a week or so, then rehab after that. It'll probably be a good four to six weeks until he's fully healed again."

"No lingering issues?" Jones asked.

"Probably not. Nothing serious, anyway. Maybe some numbness or weakness every now and then, but he should be able to make a full recovery."

Jones closed his eyes and sighed, pleased to hear the news. "Thank heavens for that." Recker went over to the counter to get a cup of coffee as Jones walked around him and sat down at the desk. "Certainly was a hairy situation we got involved in."

Recker took a sip of his coffee, not seeming too bothered or affected by the events. In fact, he seemed rather calm to Jones considering Haley was being tended to by a doctor at the moment. "Sure was."

"You don't seem very upset about what happened."

"What's to get upset about? It's the work we do, the risks we take. If it turned out differently, my mood would probably be dramatically different. But Chris will be fine. Malloy made it. The only people who turned up dead was the other guys. No use in getting all choked up over it."

"I think perhaps we should excuse ourselves from this arrangement we have with Vincent," Jones said. "At least over this issue he currently is involved in."

"Why?"

"Because there is no doubt this is becoming a turf war. Something we do not need to concern ourselves with. This person challenging Vincent appears to be very dangerous and I highly doubt will be going away soon. We must be cautious. And, if I might add, if it becomes known you're helping Vincent, and killing them, it will put you directly in their crosshairs. I'm not sure that is an additional enemy we need to make at the current time."

"Maybe. But we're already involved. We already gave Vincent our word."

Jones had thoughts about giving more of an argument against continuing to help, but then thought better of it. He knew he would only be wasting his breath. Recker would never go for pulling out of the deal at this point, especially after what happened to Haley. Instead of talking about the case, Jones diverted the discussion elsewhere.

"I suppose this will affect your vacation plans now."

"Huh?" Recker said.

"Well, if Chris is on the shelf for six weeks, then you'll have to postpone your plans with Mia."

"Oh great. I hadn't even thought of that. Now she's gonna think I'm getting cold feet about it or something."

"I'm sure if you tell her what happened she'll understand."

"We'll see."

"I think I might be getting closer to finding out who's responsible for all this," Jones said.

"You've got him?"

"Not yet. But I think by tomorrow I might have the answer."

"How?"

"Do you forget the parameters by which we were working with before you did this old west shootout?"

"Oh. Yeah, I guess I did a little," Recker said.

"Speaking of the shootout, I suppose this will garner headlines and front page news."

"Yeah, but it won't come back to us."

"You're sure about that, are you?" Jones asked.

"Don't see how it could. The only people involved are either dead, wounded, or hiding from the police, anyway. Who's talking?"

"You're positive there were no other witnesses?"

"I can't guarantee anything, but I don't see who else would be there."

"Let's hope you're right."

"Should we get down to work?" Recker asked, ready to get to the next chapter of this incident.

"I think you've been through enough in one night. Take the rest of the night off. We're not burning the midnight oil here. Mia's probably at home waiting for you by now, anyway."

Recker looked at the time and saw it was approaching one in the morning. "She was covering part of someone else's shift, so she got done at midnight."

"Haven't told her about any of this yet I take it?"

"No, not yet."

"Well, go home, get a good night's sleep," Jones said. "Don't worry about getting back here until ten-ish."

"Why so late?"

"Because if I am correct in thinking I can locate the mysterious person we're looking for then tomorrow might be another long day. Get the rest while you can."

"Gee, can't wait. Maybe we can end the day with another bang."

10

Once Recker got home, Mia was already curled up in bed sleeping. Recker joined her and went right to sleep. When she finally did get up, it was after eight, and she was a little surprised to see her boyfriend still sleeping next to her. It was very unusual for him to still be in bed at that time, though she didn't know exactly what time he came home. She got out of bed and made breakfast, finally waking him up at nine o'clock.

"Wake up, sleepy," she said, playfully tapping him on the shoulder.

Recker laid there for a few minutes, looking like he was having a hard time moving.

"Have a rough night?"

"Yeah."

Mia's playful expression slowly turned to one of concern as she pulled the covers off him and started inspecting his body for bruises, cuts, or bullet holes. She ran her hands up and down his body, thankfully not finding anything.

"Looking for something in particular?" Recker asked.

"Signs of injury."

"Can I ask why?"

"Well you tell me you had a rough night, you're still in bed at nine o'clock, and you seem to be having a tough time moving. All very obvious signs of serious injury," Mia answered.

"I'm fine. I'm not the one who needs worrying."

"What's that supposed to mean?"

"Chris got hit last night."

"Oh no. Is he OK?"

"Got it in the leg. Should be back to normal in about six weeks or so."

"Oh, thank God."

"May throw a wrench into your vacation plans," Recker said.

"I don't even care about that right now. What happened?"

Recker spent the next few minutes explaining what happened the night before in detail, not forgetting even the tiniest of details. After he was finished, Mia let out a rather loud sigh and leaned back against the headboard.

"What?" Recker asked, knowing something was bothering her.

"Just... I dunno, seems like you're getting put into tougher situations all the time."

"I've always been in tough situations. That's the job."

Mia shook her head. "I know. But it seems like you've

gotten away from helping the people that need it most. Now you're getting mixed up in a turf war between criminals you always said you wouldn't get involved with. You're not helping anyone innocent."

Recker stared straight ahead for a minute, knowing she was technically correct, things had gotten more complicated over the years since they started their operation. Things weren't as clear cut as they were in the beginning.

"It's not as easy as that," Recker said. "Things happen, relationships evolve. To do some of the things we do, sometimes we need help from people who don't always have the best of intentions. And that comes at a cost. And that cost is, sometimes, I need to get involved in situations that, on the surface, I probably should be staying clear of. Some of the happy endings we've had wouldn't have been so happy without Vincent's help."

Mia sighed again, already knowing everything he said was true, though it didn't make her feel much better about it. "I know. I just hate it when you get involved with him. I guess it's because I know whenever he's in the picture it seems like the danger factor goes up like a thousand percent. Especially when someone's after him."

Recker couldn't dispute the fact things seemed to ratchet up a notch when Vincent was involved. And he wasn't going to try to give her a bunch of fluff they both knew wasn't true to make her feel better. So, he didn't even try. He took her in his arms and hugged her for a few minutes. They spoke no more and simply let their embrace do their talking for them.

It wasn't until ten-thirty Recker finally made it into the office. Before getting there, he called Haley to make sure he was doing all right. Jones was in one of his fierce typing moments as Recker walked in, not even paying attention to his presence.

"You're late," Jones said, not even breaking stride with his typing, or looking his partner's way.

"You said after ten. You didn't say how far after. Besides, I had to check in with Chris first."

Jones stopped typing instantly and swiveled his chair around. "I called him about two hours ago and everything seemed fine. Nothing has changed I hope?"

"Nope. Still fine. Should be leaving in a couple hours."

"Great news," Jones said. "He mentioned coming back to the office after he left, but I told him to go home and relax for a bit."

"He's not gonna want to sit home and vegetate for the next six weeks."

"I'm well aware. I'm not grounding him permanently. Just for today. Then if he's up to it tomorrow, he can come into the office."

Recker then sat down at a computer and started fiddling around. "So, what can you tell me about our mysterious friend? Narrowed it down yet?"

"I've got it narrowed down to two people I believe."

"OK," Recker said. "How did you arrive at that conclusion?"

"I followed the clues."

"But there are no clues."

"You would be incorrect with that assessment," Jones

said. "Remember what we were thinking. Displaced crime bosses who have migrated in this direction."

"And how many have there been?"

"None."

Recker scrunched his eyebrows together as he lowered his head, scratching the back of it. He wasn't quite following yet. "Umm, maybe it's just me, but if there haven't been any, then how have you been able to trace someone here?"

"Relatives."

"Relatives? What's that supposed to mean?"

"While there haven't been any former bosses relocated to our area, there are two relatives of former bosses I have traced to the area."

"And they are?"

"I'd rather not say until I have pinpointed the exact person," Jones said.

"And when will that be?"

"Perhaps an hour or two."

"Want me to help?"

"No, I think I can manage on my own."

Recker threw his hands up. "So, what do you want me to do? Sit here and look pretty?"

"If you're capable of doing that."

Recker rolled his eyes but didn't say another word. As Jones went back to his work, Recker shuffled around the office, trying to keep busy. He eventually did what he normally did when he wasn't sure what else to do. He went to his gun cabinet and started cleaning his weapons. He was taking a little longer than he normally would have, finishing up in about two hours. The entire time, Recker was keeping an eye on Jones to see if he could tell when he was finished. After closing the cabinet, Recker got a drink before heading back over to the desk. He sat down next to Jones without saying anything, waiting for the professor to finish. As they were going on the third hour, Recker was starting to get impatient. He cleared his throat before talking, making sure he was loud enough for Jones to hear.

"I don't know if you know this, but we're on hour number three now," Recker said. "You're a little behind schedule."

"Better to be slow, late, and correct instead of fast, early, and wrong."

"So it is." Recker went back on the computer to keep himself busy. "But my patience is starting to wear thin."

"Patience is a virtue as they say."

"Yeah, but it's not one of mine."

Jones chuckled, though he still didn't break stride in his typing.

"How much longer?" Recker asked.

"About ten or twenty minutes."

Recker immediately looked at the time. "I'm gonna hold you to that."

"I have no doubts of that."

Only a minute later, Recker's phone rang.

"Saved by the bell," Jones said.

"It's Chris," Recker said, putting the phone next to his ear. "Yo, bud, what's up?"

"Hey, I'm good to go, so I was looking to leave in a few minutes."

"That's great."

"Yeah, but I don't have a way of getting out of here unless I hobble to a bus stop," Haley said.

"Oh, yeah, I forgot I took the car. Stay put and I'll be right there. Give me about twenty minutes."

As soon as Recker hung up, he started moving around, looking like he was about to go somewhere. Jones wasn't sure what was going on.

"Is there an issue?" Jones asked.

"What? Oh, no. Chris is ready to leave, and he's got no transport, so I'm gonna go pick him up."

"Excellent news. Just to be clear, no matter what he says, no matter how good he says he is, do not bring him back here. Take him to his apartment."

"Yes, sir. Guess that gives you some extra time and lets you off the hook too."

"Lucky me."

"I'll be back in an hour and I better get some answers by then," Recker said.

"I guess I should speed it up then."

Recker headed straight for Dr. Luke's underground offices, which weren't actually underground, but in a rather remote location. The front entrance to the facility was always closed, with bars on the windows and doors, along with blinds so no one could see inside. Anyone coming and going had to do so through the back entrance, which could only be opened from the inside. Once Recker got there, Haley was already standing outside, leaning up against the side of the building. Recker got out of the car to give his partner a hand.

"I hear you need a lift."

"Just rumors," Haley said, walking to the car with the help of crutches. Once they started driving away, Haley inquired as to their plans for the rest of the day. "So, where we heading?"

"We're heading to your apartment."

Haley sighed, not wanting to go home and rest. "I know David wants me to take the rest of the day off, but I'd rather get right back into things. I don't need to be set on the sidelines."

"It's not a punishment. You've had a rough night. He wants to make sure you don't push yourself before you're ready."

"I don't wanna sit around my apartment and stare out the window for a few weeks and do nothing."

"It won't be that long. If you're up for it, he'll probably let you back in the office tomorrow. Like I said, he doesn't want you to push it. Just relax, do what you can in the office, and do your rehab."

"I know one thing," Haley said. "I can guarantee it's not gonna take me six weeks to come back."

"Oh yeah?"

"Four at the most. A few weeks ago, I ordered one of those home gyms."

"Just don't overdo it."

After taking Haley to his apartment, Recker stayed with him for an hour or so, to make sure he was in a good frame of mind. Recker wouldn't have left him if he thought Haley was down in the dumps. Recker continued talking to him about coming back to work the next day as long as he was feeling up to it, making sure his head was still in the game. Once Recker left Haley's apartment, he immediately called Jones to let him know he was headed back to the office.

"How's Chris?" Jones asked.

"He'll be fine. Wants to come back now and get into it but I convinced him to take the day. Told him if he feels up to it tomorrow, I'll pick him up in the morning and bring him in."

"You're sure that's not too fast?"

"He wants to feel like he can still contribute and not be useless," Recker answered. "He'll be fine. I can tell you something else, he'll be back in four weeks, ready to go."

"As long as he's healthy enough."

"Speaking of ready to go, are you?"

"Am I what?"

"Ready to go. You know, with the thing you were working on you promised me would be ready by now."

"Oh, that," Jones said.

"Yeah, that." Recker got the feeling he was about to be stalled again.

"Well..."

"Jones... you told me it'd be ready."

"And it is."

"It is?"

"Yes, it is."

"Well?" Recker asked, anxious to hear the person's name.

"I think it would be better if I told you when you get back."

"You're really gonna do that to me?"

"Yes."

"Gonna keep me in suspense the entire way over there, huh?"

"If you want, I can tease you even more with it," Jones replied.

"How's that?"

"It's probably not anyone you would think of."

11

Recker almost flew into the office once he got there. He immediately took a seat next to Jones and stared at him until he was acknowledged, not saying a word. Jones slowly turned his head, a little uneasy with the icy stare being thrown his way. He turned back to his computer and tried to finish what he was working on but couldn't shake Recker's eyes burning a hole through him. Jones looked at him out of the corner of his eye, trying not to turn his head in his partner's direction.

"Yes?" Jones asked. "Something on your mind?"

"We really gonna do this again?"

Jones finally turned his head completely toward him. "Oh. The, uh, the mysterious person."

Recker gave half a smile. "Yeah. That one."

Jones picked up a file folder on the desk and handed it over to him. "Oh. Well it's all right there."

Recker looked at him like he thought he was being kidded again. "In here?"

"Promise, it's all there."

Recker still wasn't sure he was being told the truth but eagerly opened the folder and started devouring its contents. Almost immediately, his eyes bulged out, not believing what he was seeing. He brought his head up and looked at Jones, who simply nodded.

"That's correct," Jones said.

"It's a woman?"

Jones knew Recker would be a little shocked at the revelation, even though they'd run into women criminals before. "Yes. Women do commit crimes you know."

"Yes, I know, but..."

"You weren't expecting one in this instance?"

Recker shook his head. "No, not at all."

Recker continued reading the file, which was a comprehensive bio Jones had compiled on the woman. He was still a little stunned, though he knew he shouldn't have been. He'd certainly been around long enough to expect the unexpected.

"You're sure it's her?" Recker asked.

"There is no doubt. I have traced her to here. She's definitely in the city."

"You know where she is?"

"Surprisingly... yes," Jones answered. "If she's trying to conceal her current whereabouts, she's doing it badly. In saying that, my suspicion is she's not trying."

"Where is she?"

"Currently staying in a very luxurious hotel, as she has been doing for the last several weeks."

Recker took his eyes off the folder again to look at Jones. "A hotel?"

"Again, not what you were expecting?"

"No." Recker sighed, not understanding what was happening here. He didn't get why this woman would be trying to conceal her identity in trying to knock off Vincent's crew, but then stay out in the open in a hotel, which was not the actions of someone trying to hide.

Jones studied Recker's face as he read the material in the folder. He could tell Recker seemed to be having trouble digesting some of it. "What is it in particular that's giving you trouble?"

"I don't know. Nothing I guess."

"Stefania Nowak, thirty-six-years old, wife of Paul Nowak, who is now deceased as of one year ago," Jones said. "If you've gotten that far, she's made calls to Boston, New York, and Baltimore in the past six months. And who do we know from those places?"

"And the hits on Vincent's crew happens to coincide with her arrival," Recker said. "I dunno, maybe I'm just having a hard time seeing her as the head person in this. Says here her husband was in charge of an organization in Boston. With his death, she faded into the background. If this is what she wanted, why not continue with what her husband started?"

"You're assuming she, in fact, had that chance. And, according to my research, she did not. Immediately after Paul Nowak's death, the leadership changed hands to one of his captains, and that is why she faded into the background. Not any grand design by her, but because she was forced to."

"She mustn't have been that involved with the business if that's the case. Otherwise they would have kept her on in some capacity."

"Be that as it may, she may have had more of an influence in her husband's organization than anyone knew. Either she was secretly involved in the day-to-day operations, or she was taking a lot of notes, studying her husband's business in anticipation of one day taking over."

"I still don't get it, though. If that's the case, and that's her ambition, why not stay and fight for control over the business your husband started?" Recker asked.

"Perhaps she was more interested in starting something from the ground floor. Something she could put her own stamp on. Or maybe she felt like she was continuing his legacy instead of starting her own. It's impossible, at this point, to know her true motivations. Whatever they are, though, I think it's safe to say she does have some skills at this. To pull off the hit on Vincent's men, then the attempted hit last night, does require some abilities."

"So, now the question becomes; what do we do about it?"

Jones tilted his head, a little perplexed, not sure there even was a question. "To my knowledge, our little part in this is over. Complete. We were tasked with finding out who this was. We have done that."

"So, you're saying just hand everything over to Vincent

and take a step back and let whatever happens happen?" Recker asked.

"What other option is there?"

"We become proactive in this and drive her out of the city before she gets a stronghold in it." Jones made a face, obvious to Recker he didn't agree with the proposition. "You don't agree?"

"If we're talking honestly, then no, I don't."

"Our mission here is to take on the bad guys."

"No, our mission here is to help the innocent," Jones replied. "Saving one bad guy from another does not qualify."

"But if we let another criminal element into this city, more innocent people will get hurt. It's inevitable."

"Are you sure you're worried about that or is it you don't want to see Vincent replaced?"

Recker glared at him, not really liking the question, no matter how valid it was. He thought for a minute before replying. "Even if I were to admit that... it's not a case of saving him, per se. It's more the fact that in the world we live in, there's bad people in it. You're never going to have a crime-free city or society. There's going to be people who try to capitalize on the hurting of others. That's just the way it is."

"I agree with that."

"So, in admitting there will always be a criminal element, I'd rather try to keep the one that most aligns with our own interests."

"But how do you know Ms. Nowak would not?" Jones asked.

"I don't. But it's like they always say, dance with the girl that brought you. The grass ain't always greener on the other side."

"They also say don't cut off your nose to spite your face."

"How's that apply here?"

"I don't know. I figured if you could throw out a saying so could I."

"Anyway, we know we can coexist with Vincent. There's a healthy respect between us. He's largely stayed out of our way. We know we can trust him to a certain degree. He mostly stays to his own dealings and doesn't bother with business that involves us. There's no guarantee that same deal will apply to Nowak."

"Again, you're assuming a lot of things about someone we don't know," Jones said.

"Vincent also has a lot of contacts in this city, some of which have helped us. We've been able to lean on that knowledge at times. If Nowak takes over, that eliminates a source of information to us. She's not gonna have that same level of contacts and sources he does."

"But you're also assuming her and her organization will survive against Vincent. If we turn the information over to him, let him deal with it. My instincts tell me if the two factions come to battle, he will, in fact, come out on top. All without us having to get involved in it further or lift a finger in either direction."

"Guess we're in a tie here," Recker said. "Maybe we should duel it out in a cage fight or something."

"Don't be ridiculous. We'll simply talk it out like we always do until we come to a satisfactory conclusion."

"Satisfactory for who?"

"For both of us."

"There's a third member of this team now, you know."

"Of course there is," Jones said. "Don't talk to me like I'm slighting him. He's simply not here right now."

"There's one way to solve this if you're up for it."

"I'm not donning boxing gloves."

Recker laughed. "No, something much easier than that."

"I'm listening."

"Let's put it up to a three-person vote. Those in favor of staying involved and those in favor of handing it off to Vincent and stepping aside."

Jones hesitated for a second, thinking whether he was OK with however the vote turned out. He concluded he was. "Fine. If you are really on board with it."

"I am."

"No matter which way it goes?"

Recker shrugged. "No matter which way it falls, I'll hop on board."

"And we're not to tell him which way our votes fall."

"Agreed. Besides, it'll make him feel better, like he's still part of things."

Recker immediately got Haley on the line, who picked up after only one ring. Recker put the phone on speaker so Jones could hear.

"Need me back already, huh?" Haley joked.

"Well, kinda, we do have a question for you."

"OK, shoot."

"Interesting way of putting things considering your current predicament," Recker said.

"So, what's the question?"

"Well, we've found out who our mysterious player is and you're going to be the deciding factor in what we do with that information."

"How's that?" Haley asked.

"Not telling you who's voting which way, but one of us wants to stay involved in the situation to get rid of the new threat, and one of us wants to hand the information over to Vincent and let him deal with it, then walk away."

"So, whichever way I swing, one of you is gonna be mad at me, is that it?"

"Nope. David and I both agreed to let you be the swing vote. Whichever way you decide will be fine for both of us. There'll be no hard feelings or anything either way."

"A lot of pressure here."

"Don't look at it like that," Recker said. "We're all friends, nobody's gonna be mad, anything like that. We're all a team here and you get a vote in what we do since we're split."

"Sounds good."

"You wanna know the details of who this person is?"

"No."

"You don't?"

"No. Doesn't really make a difference as far as I'm concerned," Haley answered.

Though Recker didn't know for sure, he believed he was about to be disappointed with his other partner's answer. From the sounds of it, he thought Haley was about to side with Jones.

"You're sure nobody's gonna be mad at me for my answer?" Haley asked again.

"We're all friends here, Chris," Recker replied. "We're a team here and we're gonna stay that way. This isn't big enough to change any of that."

"OK. Well then my vote is to hand the information over to Vincent and step away from it."

Recker looked over at Jones, who had a slight grin on his face, happy with how the vote turned out.

"Sorry for whoever I voted against, though I have a pretty good idea who's who," Haley said.

"Out of curiosity, who do you think was which?" Jones asked.

"I'd say David voted to step away and Mike voted to keep after it. Am I right?"

"Right on the button."

"You know, I'm not sure I like how well everyone knows me," Recker said, choosing to make a joke instead of getting mad he didn't get his way.

After a few more minutes of conversation about Haley's health, Recker let him get back to resting. He immediately looked back at Jones, who seemed to be very pleased at the turn of events.

"You look pretty satisfied," Recker said.

"I must admit I am."

"You knew all along he was gonna side with you, didn't you?"

Jones put a couple fingers in the air. "Scout's honor, I had no idea."

"Scout's honor, huh?" Recker said with a laugh. "I think you did. That's why you went along with it so easily. Going to him for the tiebreaker."

Jones shook his head, still admitting to nothing. "Honestly, I had no idea. I think by now, just like I do with you, I have a pretty good idea of how Chris' mind works. He's much more level headed in his thinking than you are. No offense."

Recker smiled. "None taken."

"While he doesn't take things to the extreme that I do, he still looks at things more analytically than you do. He sees more of the big picture. My only concern was that with getting shot last night, his emotions would cloud his judgment and he would want to get back into things and hope to get some revenge."

"You know I would."

"Yes, I know. Like I said, he does not get as emotionally involved and looks at things with a more level head."

"Guess he's been everything you hoped he would be, huh?" Recker said.

"And more. I think it's fair to say he's worked out even better than we could have hoped. But in getting back to our situation, how are we going to handle it?"

Recker shrugged, thinking it was already resolved. "I thought we just voted on it."

"We did. And I guess my real question isn't how, but when?"

"Well, guess there's no time like the present. Might as well do it now. How much should I give him?"

"Give it all to him," Jones answered. "We have no more need of it or any reason to conceal any of it for our own purposes. He should be happy with it."

"I don't think happy is quite a strong enough word for how he'll feel about getting this. It'll be more like the fourth of July with fireworks going off."

"I'm sure it will be once he actually comes face-to-face with Ms. Nowak."

12

Recker called Vincent and let him know they had the name of who they believed was behind everything. Though Vincent pushed to learn the identity of the person right away, Recker was able to convince him to wait a day, until the following morning. They agreed to meet at their usual place, where Recker could turn over the contents of the folder they'd compiled on Nowak. Recker didn't want to give Vincent a name and let him go off half-cocked without having all the information at his fingertips. He wanted to deliver it in person, so Vincent knew everything he was up against.

When Recker arrived at the diner, he saw the usual guard was standing by the entrance, so he knew Vincent was already there. As Recker walked up to the door, the guard gave him a head nod.

"Ever miss the old days when we used to argue back and forth about how many weapons I had?" Recker asked.

The guard laughed. "Not really."

The two shot the breeze for a minute before he went inside. For the first time, there was nobody there to greet him. With Malloy currently out of the picture, it was a weird feeling for Recker to not see him there. He looked down to the usual table and saw Vincent sitting there. Recker walked down to it and hopped in the booth across from him.

"A little weird not seeing Malloy there," Recker said.

"Not so easy for me either."

"How's he doing by the way?"

"He's going to pull through," Vincent said. "Dr. Luke's keeping him another couple of days, then he'll be released."

"Good to hear. Why take him there, by the way? Why not a regular hospital?"

"I'm sure you of all people should understand the answer to that. People who go to medical facilities with gunshot wounds invariably invite questions. Questions I don't want answered. And law enforcement personnel I may not want to deal with. It's simpler this way. Wouldn't you say?"

"Oh, yeah, I agree. I wanted to see if your reasoning would be any different than mine."

"You said you had something for me?"

Recker plopped the file folder down and slid it across the table. "Should be everything you're looking for."

A pleased look came across Vincent's face, hoping he was finally about to learn the truth about who was coming after him. He opened the folder and eagerly started reading. It wasn't long before he perked his head back up and looked at Recker, surprised at the name.

"Stefania Nowak?"

Recker nodded. "Surprised to us too."

"Without trying to sound disbelieving, how accurate do you believe this information to be?"

"We put it at about ninety-nine percent," Recker answered.

"That's about as near a guarantee as you can get."

"It's her. Well, you'll see as you keep reading and get to the details. Ever had business with her or her husband before? Something that went sideways?"

Vincent shook his head. He periodically looked up at Recker to talk as he continued reading, soaking it all in. "No. I knew of her husband though, Paul Nowak. He was killed about a year ago."

"Why would she be targeting you? Ever take business away from them somehow?"

Vincent tossed one of his hands in the air, unsure about any past dealings. "Not to my knowledge. It's sometimes difficult to gauge how your actions will affect others. But, considering she's from a different area, I don't think our paths would have crossed very often."

"Yeah, we really couldn't find any kind of connection either. Maybe there isn't one. Could be she's just targeting you because this is a big city and you're the only major player left in it. She might think there's room for one more. Or she could think it's an easier path since there's only you, instead of going to another city where she might have to deal with multiple people."

Vincent didn't reply for a couple minutes as he stared at the information at his fingertips. His eyes couldn't read fast enough for his liking as he wanted to devour everything in an instant.

"So, what do you think you're gonna do?" Recker asked, even though he knew it was unlikely Vincent would reveal any of his plans to him.

"Tough to say right now. These things require a great deal of thought and planning. As you remember, I'm not an impetuous man. I won't rush into something that won't be to my advantage."

"Maybe she's not looking to take you out. Maybe she just wants a little piece for herself."

"There's only one problem with that," Vincent said.

"What's that?"

"As you quite honestly told me several years ago, no one is satisfied with having a little piece. Everyone eventually wants more. And if it's not dealt with appropriately at the beginning, then it becomes a bigger issue."

"So, you don't think you could possibly coexist?"

"Why would I want to coexist?" Vincent asked. "I have prevailed over the leaders of three other factions that loomed over this city for several years. Why would I want to go back in time and have to give up what I was working towards for so long?"

Recker nodded, understanding his concerns and reasons. "Makes sense. Just figured I'd ask."

"Now in saying that, it doesn't mean I will hit her immediately. It doesn't mean I will hit her at all. Perhaps I'll set up a meeting first and discuss her intentions with her. Maybe we're all worrying about nothing."

"Sounds like a good idea."

"With Jimmy out of commission for a while, maybe you could even join me for this meeting."

Recker smiled, having a feeling something like that was coming. "Yeah, I don't think that'd be possible."

"David won't allow it, huh?" Vincent said with a smile.

"Our deal was to find out who was behind this and we've done that. Our arrangement wasn't to get involved in the fight."

"Just figured I'd ask. Speaking of partners, it was nice to finally see the new one of yours. What was his name? Chris?"

Recker nodded. "Haley."

"Old friend of yours?"

"Nope. Never met him before he came here."

"He must be very highly regarded then for him to join your operation."

"He is. He's every bit as good as I am."

Vincent grinned, thinking of some unlikely possibilities regarding the new man. Recker could tell by his smile he had some thoughts in his mind.

"He's not gonna join you either," Recker said.

"Well, it was just a thought."

Stefania Nowak was in her luxurious hotel room, conducting business and making plans for her upstart organization. She knew it was likely it would eventually be discovered she was the brains behind what was happening thus far. She also knew it was likely someone would find out where she was staying. Though she was checked in under a false name, she was aware that would only provide cover for so long. In anticipation of someone coming, Nowak always had a couple of guards stationed outside the door. Nobody got in unless they were expected. She was in the middle of deciding their next route in her little crusade against Vincent. Knowing she had already bested him twice, getting one over on him both times, she knew it would only get harder from there to continue doing that. She knew by Vincent's reputation he would be more cautious from that point on.

Nowak's planning with a couple of her underlings was interrupted by a small commotion outside. It sounded like her guards were raising their voices. It could only mean they had an unexpected visitor. She started going to the door to see what was happening, but was stopped by Milton and Teasley, who didn't want her to expose herself in case something violent went down.

"We'll check it out," Milton said.

Nowak stayed in the background as Milton and Teasley went out the door. There was a man trying to approach the room, who was now face-planted on the ground, courtesy of the guards.

"What are you doing here?" Milton asked.

"Like I was trying to tell these thugs, I got a message for your boss."

"Which is who?" Teasley asked, not wanting to give away her name in case it was a trick.

"Stefania Nowak."

Milton nodded toward the two guards, one of whom had his knee on the back of the man's head. They got the man to his feet and patted him down to check for weapons.

"He's clean," a guard said.

The man, who was dressed in a suit, readjusted his clothes as he gave a nasty look to the guards who had tackled him.

"So, what are you doing here?" Milton asked.

"Like I said, I got a message for your boss."

"What is it?"

"I was told to give it to her."

"Nothing gets to her until it goes through me first."

The man shrugged, being told in advance it was likely to go down this exact way. The man then reached inside his suit jacket and removed a note, handing it over to Milton. As Milton went to grab it, the man pulled it back.

"I was told this was only to be read by Ms. Nowak."

Milton looked at Teasley, then back at the man, skeptical of what was happening. "This note isn't getting to her unless I know who it's from."

The man smiled. "It's from Vincent. He sends his regards."

Milton's face took a more concerned tone to it. "Agreed," he finally said.

The man then handed the note over again, this time letting Milton take it from him. "Be seein' ya soon." The man put his hands up to the top of his head as if he was tipping his hat, even though he wasn't wearing one, then turned around and started leaving. Milton and company stayed there for a minute and watched the man as he got on the elevator.

"A little strange," Teasley said.

"Strange ain't the word for it," Milton replied. "Well, might as well let her see whatever this is."

"Can't be good."

"We'll see."

The guards retook their stations by the door as Milton and Teasley went inside. They saw Nowak coming out her bedroom, not seemingly concerned about what was happening outside. When she saw the looks on their faces though, she had a feeling something was up.

"What was all that about?" Nowak asked.

Milton walked over to her and handed her the note. "Looks like business is about to pick up faster than we expected."

A great deal of concern overtook Nowak's face as she looked at Milton and took the note from him. "What's this?"

Milton didn't respond except for a head shake and a shrug. Nowak eagerly unfolded the paper and her eyes were immediately drawn to who the note was from rather than its contents. Once she saw it was from Vincent, the hairs on her arms stood out of nervousness as she wondered what he wanted, alarmed he already knew where she was.

Ms. Nowak,

I believe it is time for us to meet. We have a great many things to discuss. As soon as you are ready, I am at your service. At first, I thought it would be wise to have an introductory meeting at a neutral site, but then I thought, it would be better if I just came to you. Therefore, you may simply walk down to the lobby. I am waiting in the hotel restaurant.

Regards,

Vincent

Nowak's eyes widened, and, for the first time since she arrived in Philadelphia, looked nervous. This was completely unexpected and out of the blue.

"Are you OK?" Milton asked, noticing his boss' expression.

Nowak handed him the note. "He's here."

Milton read the note, looking as nervous as his boss. "What do you think he wants?"

"I don't know. It seems unlikely he would choose here as a place to hit us if that's what he had in mind. If that were the case, I'm sure he'd pick a neutral place."

"What would he have to talk about?"

"Maybe he's just here to give you a warning or threaten you," Teasley said.

"Could be," Nowak said.

"You know, you don't have to go down there," Milton said. "You're under no obligation to meet him right now. We can wait until you're ready, under your terms. This is too soon. We can sneak you out the back."

"He's sure to have men in the lobby as well as in the back. Don't believe for a second he hasn't planned for every possible reaction on our part."

"We can wait awhile. Let me call the rest of the boys and have them come over."

"And turn this hotel into a bloodbath? That doesn't help us a bit if we're all led away in handcuffs."

"So, what's the play?"

"We'll go down and meet him," Nowak answered.

"You sure? What if he tries something down there? He could have us outnumbered. Or he could try to surprise us with something."

"Maybe. But, like I said, I don't think this would be the ideal time for him to do that. If that was his goal, I doubt he'd give us the courtesy of announcing his visit first. He could have just stormed this room if that was his intent, don't you think?"

"Yeah, I guess so."

"Let's think positively for a moment," Nowak said. "Maybe he's terrified of what we're doing and wants to join forces."

"I think that's wishful thinking."

13

Within five minutes, Nowak was ready to meet her opponent. But she wasn't going alone. Milton and Teasley would accompany her, at least into the restaurant, until she saw what the setup was. Once they were all ready, they stepped out of the room into the hallway. Before leaving, she had last-minute instructions for the guards at the door, in case someone tried to sneak into the room while she was gone.

"We'll be in the restaurant," Nowak said. "Nobody is allowed to be up here."

"Right."

Nowak, along with her assistants, went to the elevator and down to the first floor. They slowly walked through the lobby, carefully looking at their surroundings to see if they thought any of Vincent's men were staked out there. They couldn't be sure, though. It was a busy night and there seemed to be a lot of people coming and going. A few people looked like they might have been lookouts, but nothing they could definitely determine.

Other than the uncertainty of the meeting, Nowak was relatively sure it would be a peaceful gathering. Going on that assumption, taking her subordinate's suggestion of leaving was not a preferable option. She knew Vincent would have people watching in back of the building. Because that's what she would do if the roles were reversed. The best option they had was listening to what he had to say.

When they finally got to the hotel restaurant, Nowak stopped in the entrance area and looked around for her host. The restaurant was packed with customers, but she found him without too much trouble. She then made a beeline for the table, her second-in-commands closely following her along the way. Vincent did have people watching in the lobby and they had already given him the heads-up Nowak was on the way, so he was aware she was coming. He kept his eyes focused on her as she approached the table.

"May I sit?" Nowak asked, almost a glow on her face as if she was meeting a date.

"Please do," Vincent replied with a smile, also sounding pleasantly happy with her presence. Based on their initial encounter, one would never know they were enemies.

After helping their boss with her seat, Milton and Teasley began to sit down. Before they reached their seats though, Vincent made sure to let them know they weren't welcome.

"This is a private meeting," Vincent told them. "There are other tables available."

They didn't really like it and looked to Nowak for guidance, who nodded at them, so they knew it was OK to leave. Once they were out of listening range, Vincent spoke.

"Thank you for meeting me on such short notice."

"I didn't think I really had much choice considering you probably have the building surrounded with your people," Nowak said.

Vincent knew that was an accurate statement, but didn't want to throw it in her face that he had the upper hand. "Well, you still could have chosen an alternate path than this one." He pointed at the glass in front of her. "I took the liberty of ordering a glass of wine for us. I hope it's an acceptable choice."

Nowak smiled, a little surprised at how gracious her host was being. She took a sip of the wine. "Not too bad."

"I'm sure I took you a little off-guard with me coming here."

"Just a little. I did not anticipate being found out so quickly. You must have good sources."

"You cannot get to the top and stay there without having good intelligence. If you're here much longer, you'll find out mine is second to none."

"I'll remember that."

"Before we get down to any business discussion, I'd like to pay my respects on the loss of your husband last year. I was sorry to hear that."

"Thank you."

"Now that's out of the way, I'd like to get down to why you're here in this city and why you've attacked me specifically."

"You certainly don't beat around the bush, do you?" Nowak asked. "Right to the point."

"It depends on the circumstances."

"As for why I'm here, it's strictly business. You're the only game in town and I believe there is a financial opportunity here."

"And it's as simple as that?" Vincent asked.

"Yes, it is."

"Then why have you attacked my men on two different occasions lately?"

"Well, if you're going to move into a new city, what better way to establish yourself than by taking on the biggest and the baddest to let everyone know who you are?"

"And you think you can just come in here, try to take me on, and bully me, and think there won't be repercussions? That I'll just take it lying down and let you operate?"

"Well I don't see any guns pointed at me," Nowak said with a smile, feeling very sure of herself.

"I think you're playing a very dangerous game here. One which you may not understand the full value of what you're up against."

"That's very disappointing."

"What is?"

"That you think of me as an ordinary woman who's in over her head," Nowak answered. "That I'm someone who couldn't possibly understand the inner workings of business. You see, I was very much involved with my husband's dealings. I watched, I learned, I listened, I attended meetings, I asked questions... I wasn't the trophy wife who was only there to brighten up the room."

"My intention was not to downgrade your capabilities, but to emphasize I am not a man to play games with."

"Oh, I'm fully aware of your reputation, Vincent. Everyone on the east coast knows who you are and recognizes your achievements. Especially how you've managed to rid this city of your enemies in the last few years. Very impressive."

"But not impressive enough to scare you away."

"Not when there's an opportunity such as this one," Nowak said.

"And you think you'll fare differently than my past enemies?"

"Well, I think I might if that's the route I chose to go. But I don't. We can work equally with one another, you know."

"You mean a partnership?" Vincent asked.

"No, nothing that extreme. Something where we acknowledge each other and peacefully coexist."

Vincent put his hand over his face and rubbed his chin as he looked at her. "Perhaps you could tell me why I'd be willing to hand over part of what I've worked so hard to achieve?"

"Because I've already shown you what I'm capable of. If it's a war you want, you can have it."

"It seems to me you've already made the first volley in that direction," Vincent said.

"Oh, come now, that was just merely me announcing my arrival," she said, flashing an innocent smile at him. "There was no harm meant to you behind it. I figured you could lose a few insignificant men at some low-level business dealings. I mean, how much could that cost you?"

Vincent had moved his hand up to his lips as his finger moved back and forth across them. He intently listened and hung on every word his guest was saying. And with each passing sentence that came out of her mouth, the more he found himself disliking her. Nowak could tell Vincent seemed to be having problems with her story and sought to help him understand.

"Listen, I don't want to have a war with you," Nowak said. "I believe it's unnecessary and wouldn't be good for either of us. My intention was not to shoot the opening salvo in a conflict with you. My only intention for this whole charade was to prove to you I am your equal."

"Then why not set up some type of meeting with me and explain your intentions?"

Nowak laughed, thinking how ridiculous it sounded. "Oh, please. Like you would have even given me the time of day if I walked into your office and we had this conversation. You would have waved me off, thinking I couldn't possibly do some of the things I say I can."

"Perhaps."

"There is enough room in this city for the two of us. For both of us to make money. That is the end goal, is it not?"

"Money is only a small part of it," Vincent answered.

"How about you tell me what you're into and I'll make sure I stay out of it? I'll only operate in things that you're not."

"Very gracious of you."

"Like I said, there's enough here for the both of us to work with; we don't have to be enemies."

"You and I both know the only way to truly operate in cities like this is to have power. And I have it. Drugs, guns, blackmail, laundering, counterfeiting, extortion, you name it; it all runs through me."

Nowak smiled, thinking he still didn't see the big picture. "There are other things to get involved in, you know."

"Even if there were, there's only so long you can operate without wanting a bigger slice of the pie. Eventually, you want more. It's human nature. I once operated in this city with two others, not because of choice, but because that's what I came into. Then there were two. Then there was one. No one is satisfied in sharing with others."

"I get the feeling you're not interested in my proposal."

"Nothing personal," Vincent said. "You seem like a very charming woman. And in another city, I'd wish you much success."

"But not this one?"

To diffuse the tension, Vincent sat for a moment, thinking of other options at their disposal. "I'll tell you what I can do for you. I'll overlook the two occasions you threw down on me."

"Very generous of you," Nowak said.

"You pack up and move to another city, start up your operations elsewhere, and I'll even give you a hand. Give you a loan, with a nice interest rate on my end, loan you men, information, resources, whatever you need to successfully get off the ground."

"Well, that is a kind offer. I'm kind of partial to mine though."

"You see, that's where you have to learn your place in the pecking order. I'm on top here. And I'm not about to let someone come in here and blast away at me then dictate terms to me with the hopes I'll just lie down and take it."

"So, my plan is being rejected?" Nowak asked, still a pleasant look on her face, not really expecting him to throw in with her.

"Rejected, torn up, and stomped on. But I do hope you'll take my offer under consideration. And because I'm a generous man, I'll give you three days to accept my terms."

"And if I choose to stay?"

"Then I'll make you wish you hadn't."

"Is that a threat?"

"Let's just call it a very stern warning," Vincent replied. He then looked at the time and excused himself. "I'm sorry for leaving so quickly, but I have other matters to attend to."

"I understand. So, how will I get in touch with you in the next few days if I decide to accept your offer?"

"Just put the word out on the street like you did your last trick. I'll hear it."

"And if you don't hear from me?"

"Then I would suggest you start traveling with more than two guards."

Vincent then stood and walked away from the table. As he walked away, about ten other men placed at various spots throughout the room also stood and soon joined him. Nowak watched as he exited the room, followed by his group of men. Milton and Teasley then joined her table.

"How'd it go?" Milton asked.

"About how we expected," Nowak answered.

"What'd he have to say?"

"Gave us a deadline of three days to get out of here. He's even willing to help us set up in another city."

"Kind of him," Teasley said.

"More than generous."

"Are we taking it?" Milton asked.

"Of course not. We're staying here. Mr. Vincent will just have to deal with it."

"Should I get Gabe to bring up the rest of the men?"

"Yes," Nowak said. "We will be needing them in short order."

"What about that other thing?"

"What other thing?"

"You know, that other guy you were talking about. That Silencer guy."

"Oh yes. He's got a big reputation around here and I wanna meet with him."

"How are we supposed to find him?" Milton asked.

"How do you find anybody? Put the word out. Talk to the right people. Do that and we'll find him."

"And what if he doesn't want to meet?"

"Then you make him want to," Nowak answered.

"Got it."

"He's a man that could help us in this upcoming war."

"And what makes you think he'll be willing to help us?"

"Money. That's what makes the world go round. Give him enough money and I'm sure he'll be willing to help us do anything."

14

Recker arrived at the office, finding both Jones and Haley banging away at the keyboard. After grabbing some coffee, he joined them at the desk.

"What's the good word, people?" Recker asked. "Find our next case yet?"

"We are working on it," Jones replied.

"How long?"

"Oh, a day or so probably. Enjoy the break."

"Who said I wasn't?"

"We know how you get when you have too much time between things," Jones said. "You start to go stir-crazy."

"How you feeling, Chris?"

"Hanging in there," Haley answered. "Better than yesterday. Oh, David told me about your vacation plans. Sorry about ruining them for you."

Recker gave him a pat on the back. "Don't worry about it."

"Is Mia mad?"

"Nah. She's more concerned that you're OK. Besides, I told her we weren't canceling plans, just pushing them back two or three weeks. She's good with that. As long as I'm not canceling them permanently. Then we might have an issue."

"Have you heard anything regarding the Vincent, Ms. Nowak issue?" Jones asked.

"I heard they had a meeting at her hotel in the restaurant two nights ago."

"Any idea how that went or what was discussed?"

"Haven't a clue. Somebody told somebody, who told Tyrell, who then told me."

"Interesting development. That's something I wasn't predicting would happen. A meeting between the two."

"What'd you think would happen?" Recker asked. "That Vincent would just go in there blasting away?"

"As a matter of fact... yes."

"You know as well as I do that's not how he operates. He waits for the right opportunity."

"Nothing like surprising your opponent when they are least expecting it," Jones said.

"Too public. Vincent will wait for the perfect time to strike. And he'll do it with a vengeance."

"Well, I hope nobody innocent gets caught up in the conflict between the two of them."

"Guess we'll see how it all shakes out."

The three of them continued working on some preliminary information on upcoming cases for a few hours until Recker's phone broke the silence and their concentration. It was Tyrell again.

"What's up?" Recker asked. "Got more on that meeting the other night?"

"Uh, no, not quite. Got something just as interesting though. Maybe even more."

"More? Well that's quite a lead-in."

"Yeah, I figured you would think so."

"So, what's up?"

"Got word on the street somebody's looking to talk to you," Tyrell said.

"Somebody's always looking to talk to me."

"Yeah, not new female crime bosses though."

"Nowak?"

"Yes, sir."

"She wants to talk to me?" Recker asked.

"That's the word."

"Who says?"

"Got it from the same source who told me about that abandoned building thing the other night."

"So, it's pretty solid."

"I'd say so."

"Any idea what it's about?" Recker asked.

"Don't know. But what does anyone want to talk to you about? Help. They all recognize who you are and your place here, and they all want you on their side of things. Just the way it works."

"So, she wants to recruit me against Vincent?"

"That'd be my guess. You want me to get word back to her somehow?"

"No, I don't think that's necessary."

"What're you gonna do?" Tyrell asked.

"Maybe I'll pay her a surprise visit."

Tyrell laughed. "How did I know you were gonna say something like that? You would."

"No use in changing how I operate, right?"

"Yeah, if you say so."

"Got anything else for me?" Recker asked.

"You need more?"

"I'm always looking for more."

"Yeah, well, you're gonna have to look on another day."

After Recker finished his conversation with Tyrell, he put the phone back in his pocket. Though he didn't immediately look at his partners, he could almost feel the heat of their eyes staring at him. He slowly turned his head and saw both Jones and Haley with their eyes glued on him.

"Something I can do for you two?" Recker said.

"For starters, you can tell me why you feel the urgent need to meet with Stefania Nowak," Jones replied.

"Who said I was doing that?"

"You did."

"I did?"

"You said her name, then you said something about her wanting to meet with you."

"Oh."

"Doesn't take a genius to figure it out," Jones said.

"Tyrell said she's looking to talk to me."

"Why?" Haley asked.

"He thinks she's probably looking to recruit me somehow in her war against Vincent," Recker answered.

"Sounds about right."

"I thought we came to an agreement the other day about us staying out of this thing," Jones said.

"We are. I'm not getting involved."

"Well if you're planning on meeting with her, then I would say that is getting involved. Tell me why you're seriously considering this? What purpose does it serve?"

"There's a new player in town, possibly a major and dangerous one, and I think it would behoove us in our business to see what she's all about," Recker said.

Jones put his elbow on the table, then dropped his head into his hand and shook his head, knowing Recker was going to meet with the woman anyway, no matter how many objections he had.

"Why do I even bother?" Jones said to himself.

"What's that?" Recker asked.

"Oh, nothing. Can I ask another question even though I realize it will probably fall on deaf ears?"

"Never stopped you before."

"What happens if she is looking to take you out for whatever reason?"

"Why would she do that?"

"I don't know. Maybe because she's heard you help Vincent from time to time," Jones said. "Or maybe because she knows you were at that building the other night and is angry you got in her way and disrupted her plans. Could be any number of reasons."

"All valid reasons not to go."

"But you will anyway."

"Curiosity usually gets the better of me," Recker said.

"I'm painfully aware."

Recker then grabbed his gun and held it in the air. "Don't worry, I won't go in empty-handed. I'll be ready if something goes down."

"You don't think they're actually going to let you meet her armed, do you? They will surely pat you down first."

"Surely."

"Well then?"

"I'm not giving up my weapons."

"Oh, that should go down well," Jones said.

"We'll see."

Recker then looked at Haley. "Feel like getting out of the office for a bit?"

"What'd you have in mind?" Haley replied.

Recker grinned. "I got a little something."

Upon hearing that, Jones moved his hand over his eyes, really not liking where this was heading. "You're not seriously contemplating taking him back out into the field already, are you? I mean, he can't move quickly enough if something happens."

"For what I have in mind, moving won't be necessary. He'll be safe and stationary the entire time."

"Why do you do this to me?" Jones asked.

"Do what?"

Jones started patting his pockets as if he was looking for something. "Give me heartburn, headaches, high blood pressure." After a minute, he found some aspirin.

"Relax. It'll work out."

Recker went over to his gun cabinet and opened it, looking for a specific weapon. He pulled out a rifle with a laser scope on it. He then walked over to Haley and handed it to him.

"You'll need this," Recker said.

Haley smiled, thinking he understood what his partner had in mind. "When you wanna do this?"

"No time like the present."

Jones knew it was going to happen and didn't see the point in arguing against it any further. Now he could only hope nothing went awry.

"Let me know when it's over so I know you're both not dead in a ditch or a gutter somewhere," Jones said.

"You always have such an eloquent way of phrasing things," Recker replied.

"As do you."

Recker and Haley left the office to go to Nowak's hotel. Along the way, Recker explained his plan in detail so Haley would know what he had in mind.

"You sure that room will be available?" Haley asked. "How do you know there's a spot there?"

Recker smiled. "I've actually been to that hotel before, so I already know the layout."

"What'd you go there for?"

"A couple years ago, a businessman who had some questionable business practices was on the wrong side of a hit for hire."

"You stop it?"

"Yeah."

When they finally got to the hotel, they immediately went to the floor Nowak was staying. Once they stepped off the elevator, Recker and Haley went their separate ways. All the rooms faced each other, as there was a big balcony that encompassed the inside part of the hotel. They immediately knew which door was Nowak's, as the guards standing in front of it gave it away. With Recker approaching them, nobody paid much attention to the guy on crutches who was walking on the far side of the floor, directly across from them. As Recker got within a few feet of them, one of the guards put his hands up to prevent him from coming closer.

"Hold up, man, that's as far as you get here."

"I think I'm expected," Recker said.

"I wasn't informed of that."

"Well, tell them I'm here."

"And who are you supposed to be?"

"I'm told I'm The Silencer. I'm also told your boss was looking to meet me."

"Oh," the guard said, his face looking a little awestruck, clearly hearing of Recker's reputation beforehand.

The two guards looked at each other for a moment, neither of whom seemed to be sure what to do next.

"How about one of you go in there and tell someone I'm here?" Recker said. "That way we're not standing out here all day."

"Wait here," the guard said, ducking inside the room.

"I'll wait here."

The guard looked back at Recker, giving him a glance that indicated he wasn't amused by the quip. As he waited, he put his finger on his ear, pretending to be cleaning it out to not give away Haley's voice was coming through on the com.

"I'm in position," Haley said.

As soon as he said that, Recker quickly twirled around to look at where he was, giving the illusion he was looking at the features of the hotel. Haley had taken up residence in a maintenance room located across from Nowak's room. The room was always locked, but with the guards paying more attention to Recker, no one noticed Haley was picking the lock. He left the door open a crack to give his rifle enough room to point at the guards. He stayed just inside the door, making sure the rifle didn't stick out of the door to not give himself away if anybody was walking nearby.

A minute later, the guard finally emerged from the room again, this time with Milton behind him. As Milton closed the door behind him, he looked Recker up and down to see if the description he'd heard matched the man in person. It did.

"You look about the same as I pictured you would," Milton said.

Recker smiled, not able to resist taking a small shot at the man. "Can't say the same for you. Thought you'd be bigger."

Milton also didn't look amused. "I'm sure."

"So, we gonna stand out here jabbering all day or am I gonna talk to your boss?"

"Ms. Nowak is currently in conference."

"So, are you saying she can't see me?" Recker asked.

"Maybe come back later today or tomorrow. Or leave your number and we'll contact you when she's available."

"Listen, pal, I'm busy, this is a one time offer. I didn't come here to be poo-pooed and given the runaround by the neighborhood lackey. If she doesn't see me now, I won't be back. I heard she was looking for me. I don't really give a damn if I talk to her or not."

Milton sighed and looked somewhat disgusted. "Wait here."

"I'll wait here."

Milton gave him a second look before going back inside the room again. Recker then looked at the guards and started some small talk to pass the time.

"I like the system you guys got going on here. You try to bore people to death before they get to go inside?"

Neither of the guards replied. They actually hoped he'd be out of their hair soon as they weren't particularly impressed with his personality. A couple minutes later, Milton came out of the room again.

"You're in luck, Ms. Nowak is ready to see you now."

Recker laughed. "I'm in luck? Like how you phrase things bud. You're a real charmer."

Recker started moving toward the door but was stopped by Milton, who put his hand on Recker's chest to prevent him from going in.

"No guns," Milton said.

"Excuse me?"

"You heard me. No weapons are allowed inside. We'll need to frisk you."

Recker took a step back as he balked at the request.

"You don't need to check me. I'll tell you right now; I'm carrying."

"Boss' orders. Nobody gets inside who's packing."

"Well then, that presents a bit of a problem, doesn't it? I don't meet new people I don't trust without packing."

The guards, along with Milton, stood in front of the door to block Recker's path.

"Listen, does she wanna talk to me or not?" Recker asked.

"With no guns," Milton replied.

"Well here's the deal. I either go in, guns in my possession, or I walk away never to return."

Recker could see on Milton's face he was uncomfortable sending him away. It was obvious his boss really wanted to meet him and talk to him. If not, he figured Milton would have already told him to take a hike after balking at surrendering his weapons.

"If you want, I can make this easier for you," Recker said.

"How's that?"

"You see that red dot on your shirt?"

Milton scrunched his eyebrows together, not sure what he was talking about. He looked down at his shirt, but there was no red dot. "What are you talking about?"

Right on cue, Haley aimed his rifle at Milton's chest.

"You might wanna check again," Recker said.

Milton looked down again, this time seeing the red dot. He immediately knew what it was. A nervous look came over his face as he realized he was in the crosshairs of a sniper.

"Nobody takes my guns," Recker said. "I either go in with them or I leave. I don't really have a preference which way this goes so I'll leave the decision up to you."

Milton took a deep breath, finally ready to concede his position. Nowak really wanted to talk to him, and he was under orders to make it happen, so he relented. "Fine. You can keep your guns. Just realize if something happens..."

"Then what? I'll never make it out? Somehow, I think I would. I'll give you my word, though, nothing will happen unless someone tries to kill me. Fair enough?"

Milton nodded. "Oh, uh, and can you do something about this?" Milton asked, pointing to the red dot on his chest.

Recker put his hand on his ear. "Stand down." Within a few seconds, the dot disappeared. Recker then smiled at Milton and slapped him hard on the shoulder. "Let's get this party started, huh?"

15

Recker walked into the room, Milton closely behind him. Recker looked around and saw Teasley standing watching him but didn't see Nowak. He stood in the middle of the room for about a minute, with nobody saying a word. Recker was starting to get a bad feeling about being there. In case he badly misjudged what was about to happen, he stuck his hand inside his jacket, ready to pull out his gun if the situation called for it.

It turned out to be a false alarm for him, though, as Nowak showed up only a few seconds later. But it wasn't quite the initial appearance he imagined it would be. She came out of the bathroom, her body wrapped in a thick white towel that went from her chest to her mid-thigh. She walked right up to Recker and looked him over, in a much more lustful way than Milton had done earlier. She stuck her hand out to shake hands, which Recker reciprocated.

"So, you're the famous Silencer."

"That's the rumor," Recker replied.

"A little more good-looking than I was anticipating."

"Scars are coming next week."

"And a sarcastic sense of humor. I like it."

"It's just for you."

Nowak turned to her underlings to shoo them out of the room. "Leave us. Wait outside."

Milton and Teasley looked at each other, both surprised by their boss' wishes. It was highly unusual for them to leave her alone, as they hadn't done so in any other meeting she had up to that point. And it wasn't something she previously indicated she would do when she told them about meeting Recker.

"But... he's still armed," Milton said, not comfortable leaving her alone with such a dangerous man, who still had guns on him.

"Oh, is he?" Nowak asked, looking back at Recker seductively. "Well... everyone should live dangerously at some point."

"Ms. Nowak, I don't feel..."

"I don't pay you to feel anything. I pay you to do what I tell you."

Milton didn't look pleased at following her orders but eventually did as she asked. He looked at Teasley and nodded toward the door for him to follow him out. Once the two of them were outside, Nowak looked at Recker and touched him on the chest.

"Thanks for coming."

"Curiosity gets the best of me sometimes," Recker said.

"Follow me, so we can talk. I can change at the same time."

"I can wait out here for you. If it won't be too long."

"Oh nonsense," Nowak said, grabbing his hand. "Come into the bedroom with me. I won't bite. At least, not where it shows."

Though it was against his better judgment, Recker let her lead him into the bedroom. Once in, she directed him to a chair in the corner of the room. He sat down, expecting Nowak to duck behind a screen or into the bathroom off the bedroom. He was a little stunned she dropped her towel right in front of him, exposing her plentiful assets. She was thirty-seven, but still had the appearance of a woman who might have been ten years younger. She swore it was due to all the spa treatments, creams, and lotions she religiously used. With her youthful face and good body, she hardly looked the part of an organized crime boss. And she wasn't shy about using it if it helped her get what she wanted.

Standing there in front of Recker in all her glory, Nowak sure didn't rush to put any clothes on. She put on an act of not being able to find what she wanted to wear, all in the hopes of maybe seducing the mysterious man. Recker put his elbow on the arm of the chair and put his hand up to his face as he continued looking at the naked woman in front of him, studying her every movement. But Recker wasn't watching her with a lustful eye as most men in that situation might have done. With a beautiful woman of his own waiting for him, he had no interest in desiring somebody else, no matter how good they might have looked. No, he kept his eyes on Nowak because he knew the tactic she was trying for. It must have been something she'd tried, and succeeded with, on other men. He kept watching to see if she was planning on some type of diversion. The old watch her body while she pulls a gun, or somebody comes from a different room he's not watching trick. Nowak continually looked over at her visitor, and after a few minutes, realized her plan wasn't going quite the way she hoped. She slowly started putting her clothes on, not getting any reaction out of Recker.

"So, do you have a first name or does everyone call you The?" Nowak asked.

Recker laughed, finding some amusement in the question. "My friends call me Mike. My enemies call me Mr. Silencer."

This time it was Nowak's turn to laugh. She really enjoyed his sense of humor. Standing there in black lingerie, she hoped Recker was beginning to change his opinion on what might happen, though she had a feeling she was failing with her objective.

"So, before I get fully dressed is there anything you'd care to do or discuss before we get down to business?" Nowak asked, a slight seduction in her voice.

"I can't think of a thing, can you?"

Nowak looked extremely disappointed in his lack of interest and continued dressing, which consisted of pants, heels, and a revealing blouse. Once she was done, she walked over to the bedroom door.

"Well, if there's nothing else you can think of doing in here, would you follow me out to the main room?"

"I'd be delighted," Recker said.

Nowak stopped in the middle of the room and turned around to face him. "Well, if I can't interest you in anything spicier, can I offer you a drink?"

Recker put his hand up. "No, thank you."

"Do you always play everything straight down the line?"

"Only in the presence of strangers."

"I was hoping we could get to know each other more deeply and in more detail."

"Why?"

"I'm told you have a large, looming presence in this city," Nowak answered. "And considering I'm planning on being here a while, I figured you and I should get to know each other more intimately. You wouldn't have a problem with that, would you?"

"Some people might."

Nowak rubbed her finger across Recker's chin briefly before making her way to the bar area. "So, you have a girlfriend, do you?"

"A good man doesn't kiss and tell."

Nowak smiled. "Fair enough. You're obviously devoted to her. Like a good man should be."

"I don't mean to rush things along here, but I really didn't come here for you to analyze me. I heard you were looking for me, so here I am. How about we just stick to the business aspect of this?"

"Well if you would rather be boring about it," Nowak said, walking from behind the bar to a chair. "I always like to mix business with pleasure."

"Not me."

"So I'm gathering." Nowak pointed to a big white chair across from her. "Come sit, so we can discuss... business."

Recker complied with her wishes and sat. Up to this point, he wasn't very intrigued and was beginning to think he'd made a mistake in coming. He wasn't sure there was anything she could tell him that would have made him think otherwise.

Nowak took a sip of her drink. "So, why do you think I asked you to come here?"

"I assume you want me to help you get rid of Vincent."

Nowak smiled, not very surprised at how perceptive her guest was. "I can offer you a great deal."

"I'm sure you can. Is that it?"

"Of course not. As I'm sure you know, I have not been in town very long and I'm still figuring out the game here. Now, I already know pretty much all I need to know about Vincent. I know what he's into, the people in his pocket, and the things he does."

"You sure about that?" Recker asked, not believing she did, knowing Vincent as well as he did. "I've found he's a man you really can't count on for knowing anything about."

"Well, I may not know every single little detail about everything he does, but I know what I need to know. What I don't know is how you fit into it?"

"I don't."

"Oh, well that's fantastic, because I've heard from some of my moles on the street that you and he have a very close relationship."

"In a few instances our business interests have aligned," Recker replied. "We're not friends, we're not partners, we are not anything together. I do my own thing."

"I'm delighted to hear it."

"Why? Planning on making me an offer?"

Nowak grinned. "You are well-versed in the game, aren't you?"

"I didn't just graduate hitman school yesterday."

"So, since you two aren't intertwined at the hip, as they say, would you be interested in a proposition?"

Recker smiled. "Never on the first date."

"I'm sure if we were to come to some type of agreement, I could make it extremely worth your while."

"Why does that not surprise me? And just what type of agreement are you looking to make?"

"Well..."

Recker didn't mind engaging in an evasive question-and-answer session from time to time, especially since he was used to it in talking to Vincent, but he wasn't interested in continuing it this time. "Instead of this runaround conversation we're having, why don't you tell me what you really want?"

"Tell me, is it all business with you all the time?"

"Mostly."

"Your reputation paints you as one of the best," Nowak said. "Somebody who's not to be messed with. They say if there's a fight on your hands, you want The Silencer guarding your back."

"Well I don't know who 'they' are, but my cooperation in any matter depends on a variety of factors."

"Which are?"

"I have my own criteria which I choose not to divulge," Recker answered. "I also don't get involved in disputes between rival crime families."

"Well, that's disappointing to hear. May I ask why?"

"Because I'm not interested in choosing sides. I'm not here to help you or him exert your power or influence or help you make money. I'm here to help prevent innocent people from getting hurt by people like you."

"What are you? A saint or an angel or something?"

"Hardly. Just someone who tries to do the right thing."

"Sometimes the right thing can be influenced by a sizable check," Nowak said.

"Not with me. Don't give a hoot about money."

The two talked for a few more minutes, Nowak continually trying to break him down into at least considering joining her side. The more they talked though, the more she began to realize it was a worthless pursuit. Nothing she did or said seemed to interest him. She couldn't interest him with her body or her money. He was quite the unusual man in her estimation. Since he had shot down everything she had to offer so far, and since she badly desired his help, Nowak figured she'd basically let him write his own check.

"How about we do this? You tell me what you want or what interests you, and I'll see what I can do?"

"Just like that, huh?" Recker replied.

"Why not?"

Recker was silent for a few moments, trying to think of an answer for her. There was nothing he could come up with though. "I'm afraid that's a question I can't really answer."

"You can take a few days to think about it if you wish. I aim to please."

"No, it's not that. It's just there's nothing you could offer me that would persuade me to join your side or get involved in this conflict at all."

Nowak flashed a smile, though underneath it was a temper she was beginning to lose. She was able to control it though. "So, tell me, if you're not interested in anything I have to offer, or anything I have to say, why did you agree to come here?"

"I'm always interested in meeting new people I might come across one day."

"So, you're leaving the door open to us working together at some point?" Nowak asked.

"Nope. I'd say it's unlikely. I'll just give it to you straight. After today, I hope I never run into you again. And whatever your plans are for being in this city, I'd like to stay out of them. I'm here for one reason and one reason only and that's to protect the innocent. Whatever game you have going on with Vincent or any other criminal doesn't really concern me."

"Straight down the line."

"If we ever see each other again, it's likely because you knocked over the neighborhood grocery store or worked over an old man walking down the street or trying to intimidate a law-abiding person into doing something illegal that benefits you. If any of those are the case, then we'll be seeing each other again real soon."

Nowak nodded, finally seeing the man in front of her couldn't be bought with anything she was trying to sell. "So, you're trying to tell me you and Vincent have come to that same understanding?"

"Vincent and I have learned to stay out of each other's way. I don't get involved in any of his dealings as long as innocent people aren't caught up in it, and he doesn't do anything that might cause me to stop it."

"A nice, neat arrangement."

"Has been so far."

"So, maybe you and I could come to that same arrangement," Nowak said.

"I don't see why not. I'm not looking to make enemies, just telling you how things are here."

"I understand. I only hope my relationship with you will eventually be a little closer than the one you have with Vincent."

Recker looked at her with a sharp eye and grinned, wondering if she ever stopped with the double entendres. In his view, she was obviously a woman who wasn't used to hearing the word no. He figured she was used to men doing whatever she wanted, for whatever the reason, and jumping at the chance to please her... in any situation. But she was learning he was someone who stood with his own convictions. In analyzing him, Nowak assumed he was someone who would rather go down with the ship than to do something against his own principles. Those were the types of people that usually gave her trouble.

She knew she would have to keep her eyes on him and stay guarded.

They conversed for another twenty minutes, Nowak continually probing him on more personal questions he kept evading. Recker knew her game. She was trying to find out everything she could about him in the hopes of using something to her advantage against him. Anything she could find that she could potentially use in the hopes of luring him to her side of the equation. But with his background of working in the city the last few years, plus his time in the CIA, he was well-versed in this kind of information gathering. He was easily able to brush her inquisitions aside.

"You know, I get the impression there's more to you than meets the eye," Nowak said.

"Now what gives you that idea?"

"You're a mysterious man. You stick to a certain set of ideals and don't deviate from them. You have a demeanor about you that suggests there's something else that lies beneath that rugged exterior."

"Everyone has a past and skeletons in the closet."

"Indeed, we do. But some are more interesting than others. What did you do before coming here?"

"What makes you think I did anything?" Recker asked.

"Because everybody was something else once."

"It's nothing worth mentioning in my case."

"I can't believe that to be true."

"Well, I guess we'll just have to leave it at something that's for me to know and you to find out. You seem to like playing games enough to do that."

Nowak smiled. "I think we've got a good under-standing of each other. At least to start with."

"I would say so."

"Perhaps we could meet again under less formal circumstances," Nowak said, sticking her chest out to give Recker a better view of it.

Recker wouldn't take the bait though. "No, I don't think we could."

16

I t'd been several days since Recker's meeting with Stefania Nowak. The city was a relatively quiet place since then, at least as far as gangland business went, as nobody had turned up dead yet. That was about to change, though, and in a big way. It was release day for Jimmy Malloy. He was finally being let go from Dr. Luke's care, and since he was the number one man, Vincent was showing up personally to welcome him back. Unbeknownst to him, Malloy was going to get another welcoming party, a larger and more unfriendly one.

Dr. Luke helped walk Malloy out of the back of the building, with Vincent on the other side of him. There was a black Cadillac parked only a few feet away, and the driver got out the car to assist Malloy into it. As the driver scurried around the back of the car, another car zoomed in, screeching to a sudden stop. Vincent looked wild-eyed as he suspected what was going on. Only a second later, the windows of the car went down and guns appeared in its place. The automatic rifles opened fire at the bunch, not seemingly aiming at a specific target. Vincent pushed Malloy down to the ground and stayed on top of him as the driver began to return fire. Dr. Luke started to run back toward his office but was hit in the back with several shots, dropping him to the ground long before he got there. Vincent's driver was able to hit the car with a couple of shots, though he did no real damage, and he didn't hit any of the occupants either. As the exchange of gunfire continued, the driver suddenly went down, a barrage of bullets entering his body. Once he was out of the way, the mysterious car squealed its wheels and turned around, going out the same way they came in. Vincent saw their attackers leave by observing the vehicle underneath his own car. When he knew they were out of the picture, he finally got back to his feet, and helped Malloy up to his.

"You OK?"

Malloy brushed himself off and checked for new holes in him. "I think I'm good."

"You sure? Anything hurt or anything?"

Malloy held his rib cage area, but mostly because it was still sore from the previous slugs taken out. "No, just a little sore. I'll be alright."

With him taken care of, Vincent then turned and saw his driver lying on the ground, in a pool of his own blood. Vincent knelt, not seemingly caring about getting blood on his pants, and touched the head of his former employee. The man had been with Vincent for almost ten years and was a valued member of his organization. He would be missed. Malloy then tapped his boss on the arm and pointed at Dr. Luke. Vincent was saddened at the sight of the fallen doctor. Vincent got up and walked over to him, hoping by some miracle he was still alive. Vincent observed three bullet holes in the doctor's back and knew no miracle would be arriving on this day.

"What do you wanna do?" Malloy asked.

Vincent got on his phone and made a call to the police department and one of the detectives on his payroll. He wanted to make sure it was one of them who rolled on the call. He didn't want to be dealing with a lot of unnecessary questions that would accompany a detective who didn't have that relationship with him. He was sure somebody probably heard the shots and called it in to the cops already, and though he didn't plan on sticking around at the scene, as soon as the driver was identified, somebody in uniform would be showing up at his door. He hoped to avoid that whole predicament.

Once he was done with his phone call, Vincent helped Malloy into the passenger seat of the car. Vincent then hopped into the driver's side and left the area, only a few minutes before a patrol car showed up. Silence filled the car for several minutes as the two men steamed over the loss of the two men they left behind. Both were valued and trusted men. It was something Vincent would not let pass as easily as he did the first hit against him.

"Who do you think it was?" Malloy asked.

"I don't think it's something we really have to guess on. We know who it is. We know who's behind it. A very unfortunate and misguided woman."

Recker arrived in the office, still talking on the phone. His phone had been blowing up all day from sources he had on the street, including Tyrell. But the topic of conversation was all the same. They were all telling him about the attempted attack on Vincent at Dr. Luke's office. As he reached the desk, he hung up, ready to talk about the events with the team. Jones wasn't sure if his partner had heard the news yet and was eager to discuss it. Jones dropped what he was doing as he turned toward Recker.

"It appears we have a delicate situation on our hands."

"Murder and attempted murder are usually not all that delicate," Recker said.

"So, you've heard the news, I take it?"

"I've heard about it so often already my ears are ringing."

"What're we gonna do?" Haley asked.

Recker looked away as he shrugged, not really having an answer. "I didn't know we were gonna do anything. I thought we had a vote a few days ago to stay out of this thing."

"I guess it seems more real now."

"Well, we all knew that, barring an agreement between those two, this day was coming."

"It would appear that agreement did not materialize," Jones said.

"Understatement of the year."

"I would say the only thing for us to do is continue to

monitor things, make sure it doesn't spill out into unintended places."

"If it does, then we'll intervene," Recker said. "But not before."

Nowak was pacing around in her hotel room, acting somewhat nervously, which was uncharacteristic for her. She usually seemed much more confident. But it'd been a week since the attempted hit on Vincent and Malloy and there'd been no response in the form of retaliation. It was not what they had counted on or planned when dreaming up this scenario. Nowak and her cohorts were counting on them fighting back and exposing themselves even further, opening themselves up for bigger hits and damage upon their organization.

"I don't understand what's happening," Nowak anxiously said, smoking a cigarette. "Why is he staying silent?"

"Maybe he's just waiting," Milton replied.

"Waiting for what? To get picked to pieces? To die slowly? Our contacts haven't dug up a single thing about them planning anything? What are they doing, just crawling into a hole somewhere hoping this will blow over?"

"He does have a reputation for not rushing into things," Teasley answered. "Could be he's planning something big. Something that would take a while to plan."

"Such as what? Blowing up the hotel with me in it? He wouldn't dare be so bold."

"Speaking of which, when do you plan on moving operations?" Milton asked. "Can't stay in this hotel forever."

"I'm comfortable here. I also know Vincent is not going to be so daring as to try to take me out here. There's safety out in the open. It's when you cross into the shadows that things happen. He's not going to try something in full view of everybody and draw attention to himself. Me moving is probably exactly what he's hoping for."

"I dunno. People get murdered in hotels all the time. I don't think it's above him to try it."

"Well that is why I pay for security, is it not?" Nowak asked.

"I say we keep on hitting him while we got him reeling," Teasley said. "Let's keep up the pressure."

"And what exactly do you have in mind?"

"Let's attack every building he owns. Businesses, warehouses, facilities, men, everything. Let's hit him a couple times a day until he's extinct or so scared he never shows his face above ground again."

Nowak paced around the room for a minute as she thought about it. She started moving her head around, indicating that she was in support of the action. She then stopped her pacing and sat down, eventually agreeing with the move.

"Start making preparations," Nowak said. "Draw up a plan of which buildings to hit and when. I want a precise plan. Dates, times, people involved, everything. And I want it by tomorrow."

"I'll get on it right away," Teasley replied. "I'll leave now and do some scouting. I'll have something for you tomorrow."

"Good."

Teasley left the room as he embarked on his mission to scout some of Vincent's known business locations. After he left, Nowak and Milton continued talking about the plan.

"What do you think?" Nowak asked. "Will it work?"

"I think it's good. I know you originally wanted to try to draw him out and get him that way, but I don't think that's gonna fly. He's too smart for that. He knows you'd be expecting him to retaliate. That's why he's not. He's trying to wait you out. Let you get impatient and make a mistake."

"Well then we'll just have to make sure his mistake is in not trying."

When Teasley made it down to the lobby, he kept his head on a swivel, as all Nowak's men did nowadays, since they were on the lookout for any of Vincent's faction. As he stepped through the main doors, he waited outside for a few seconds, cognizant of any cars that might be in the area. He almost expected a car to drive by, roll down its windows, and start blasting away at him. He put his hand inside his jacket and placed his fingers on his gun, thinking he may have cause to use it as he walked to his car. He was a little surprised, though not disappointed, he got to his car without incident.

Before starting his car, he pulled up the maps on his phone and plugged it into the car charger. He pulled out a small book and plugged in a couple addresses into the map app for directions. He then reached into his pocket and pulled out his keys and put them into the ignition. Teasley took a quick look out the window to make sure nobody else was around then started the car. Almost instantly after the engine turned on, the car exploded, resulting in a massive fireball shooting up into the air. The windows on each of the cars next to it shattered from the impact. Pieces of Teasley's car were torn off the vehicle and landed all over the parking lot. There wasn't much left of either the car or Teasley. What was left of the car was still on fire. There were more explosives used than were actually needed, but Vincent wanted to make a powerful statement.

The blast could be heard by everyone within the hotel and probably a couple miles beyond it. As soon as they heard the massive explosion, Nowak and Milton ran to the window. They opened the blinds completely and stared out the window, their eyes instantly drawn to the burning car they immediately knew was Teasley's. Nowak's jaws tightened as anger started boiling inside her.

"You were wondering why there was no response yet?" Milton said. "I'd say he's answered with a certain kind of flare."

"I would say the game is now in full force."

"Should we go down there and check it out?"

"Why?" Nowak asked. "There's nothing we can do down there."

"What do you wanna do now?"

"We'll do as we just discussed. We'll start hitting Vincent in spots all across the city. We'll do it in random areas, so he won't be able to pick out a pattern and be ready for us. We'll have his head spinning so fast he won't know what's happening or where we'll be next."

"I'll start working on it tonight."

They continued staring out the window at the wreckage as they talked of their plans, observing a burgeoning crowd down below. A little to the left of the blast, Nowak saw a couple men just standing there, looking up at the hotel. Though she couldn't see their eyes at that distance, by the positioning of their heads, she knew they were looking at her. She was a little shocked at their appearance, even though she probably shouldn't have been. She kept her eyes fixed on the pair, wondering if there were about to be any other fireworks soon to be set off.

"They're here," Nowak said.

"What?"

"Vincent and his goon. They're here."

Milton put his hand on the window. "What? Where?"

"To the left of the car. Just standing there. Looking at us."

"I'll get the boys ready," Milton said, about ready to rush off and tell some of the others.

Nowak put her hand on his forearm to prevent him from leaving. "Don't bother."

"What if that was just for starters? Maybe they have more planned."

"It's not."

"How do you know?"

"Because they wouldn't still be standing there if there was more to come," Nowak answered.

"What do you suppose they're doing there? Just standing."

Nowak sighed. "Sending me a message."

"Maybe we should send one back."

"We will. In time."

All parties concerned stood in their respective spots for a few more minutes, continuing their staring contest. It was almost as if each side was waiting for the other to blink and step away first. With Vincent still staring up at the window, Malloy started tugging at his boss to leave the scene, figuring someone would start connecting them to the blast.

"We should probably get going," Malloy said, grabbing his boss' arm.

"Yeah, you're right. I just wanted to make sure she got the message."

"I think it'd be pretty hard to ignore."

"Yeah, I guess you're right."

With his underling tugging at him, Vincent finally capitulated and stopped staring at the hotel and walked back toward their own car. Just before getting in, they stopped, Malloy wanting to get Vincent's thoughts on what happened.

"What do you think they'll do in response?" Malloy asked. "I'm sure they'll have one."

"Oh yes. They'll have a response. You can count on that."

"What do you think it'll be?"

"I would suspect they'll try to hit us again," Vincent replied. "Make sure you put everyone on high alert."

"Will do."

"Every man, every building, every car, everything. Might be tomorrow. Might be in a week. But you can be sure it'll be coming."

"With all due respect, sir, I think you're being too generous."

"In what way?" Vincent asked.

"Giving them a chance like this. Instead of letting them get a chance to regroup and hit us again, we should keep after them. Take it to them while they're on their heels."

"A sound strategy Jimmy. We'll take it under advisement."

"A beautiful day, sir?"

Vincent smiled and looked up at the sky. Even though there was no sun and it was a bit of an overcast day, it didn't much matter to him. It was perfect as far as he was concerned. "Yes, Jimmy, I'd say it was a beautiful day indeed. A very beautiful day."

17

A few more weeks passed, with both Vincent's and Nowak's organizations taking shots at each other. Several men on both sides were killed, though neither launched a full-out war on the other. They were both being cautious in how they approached the situation. From Nowak's perspective, she never wanted a full-scale battle with Vincent, anyway. Her approach was more one of respect. She wanted Vincent's respect that they could share the city without him losing much, if anything. At this point, she wasn't interested in taking him out. Nowak wanted him to know she was as tough as he was and she wasn't leaving without a fight. That was why she held back a little. She didn't think an all-out war with Vincent would be good for anybody. And she wasn't certain it was one she could win. At least, not yet. Not until she had some time to build up her organization, both in terms of men and money.

For Vincent, he didn't consider Nowak's organization to be much of a threat. At least not a major one. Though she showed some guts up to that point and wasn't backing down yet, he still believed the waiting game would pay off, as it usually did. He knew she didn't have as much power within the city as he did and couldn't afford a long engagement. He figured time was on his side. Rushing was where men made mistakes. And he figured that would be his undoing. He also wanted to avoid a full-out war as he knew that meant he would probably lose a good amount of men and resources. War between two factions was rarely good for anybody. Everyone took casualties. Vincent was trying to avoid that if possible. He hoped that eventually Nowak would see that he wasn't relinquishing any control or letting her set up shop within his territory and she'd pack up and leave. It would be a standstill.

For Recker and the team, not much had changed since the war between Vincent and Nowak started. They hadn't been dragged into anything, and, so far, nobody innocent had gotten caught up in their entanglements. But they had a feeling that wouldn't last forever. Eventually, someone who wasn't involved in the deal would get hurt.

They'd been working on a case involving an investment banker who looked to be engaging in some fraudulent activity and Recker was ready to make his move on the guy. Jones intercepted some text messages indicating the banker, Todd Brinson, was meeting with a contact at an outdoor restaurant in the downtown area. Recker was already at the restaurant sitting by himself and eating his meal when he saw Brinson arrive.

"Looks like our guy is here," Recker said into his com.

"Is there anyone with him yet?" Jones asked.

"Not yet."

Jones looked at the time and saw it was five minutes to one, the scheduled meeting time. "We still have a few minutes."

Recker kept his eyes fixed on Brinson, who took up a seat several tables in front of Recker, watching his every movement. The banker looked a bit nervous, looking in every direction. Recker assumed he was looking for his visitor. Five minutes passed and there was still no sign of anyone. It appeared to Recker that Brinson was starting to sweat as he was dabbing his cheeks and forehead with a napkin.

"This guy's looking really nervous," Recker said.

"Still no sign of anyone?" Jones asked.

"Not yet." Recker looked across the street and saw a familiar face walking across it. He kept his eyes fixed on the man as he came over to the restaurant and sat down across from Brinson. "Guys, we have an interesting situation here."

"What's happening? Have we finally identified the person he's meeting? Is the other party there yet?"

"Oh yeah. He's here."

"Well who is it? Do we know him?"

"Gabriel Hernandez," Recker replied.

Jones was very surprised to hear the name. "Hernandez? What is he doing there?"

"Without knowing details, and if I had to guess, I'd say

maybe we know how Stefania Nowak is funding her operation."

"Now the question is whether Mr. Brinson is a willing participant or if he's being blackmailed or coerced somehow."

"I'll find that out real quick."

"How do you plan to do that?"

"Ask him," Recker said.

"I'm not sure that's wise. If he is a willing participant in this endeavor, then introducing yourself and talking about it could blow the case sky high. He might clam up and we'll never know where it leads."

"Oh, I think we do."

"Just because Hernandez is there does not necessarily mean it's tied to Nowak. He could be operating independently of her on this deal."

"With people like Vincent and Nowak, they don't employ people who act independently of them," Recker said. "They want people to fall in line. They won't do something unless they're told to."

"Perhaps you're right, but I'm still not sure showing yourself is the right move."

"Guess we'll find out."

Jones sighed and rolled his eyes as he turned to Haley, who was sitting beside him. "Why do I even bother?"

Haley laughed. "He's usually right."

"Yes, but let's not admit that too often. He'll be even harder to live with than he is now."

Since they were at an outdoor restaurant, Recker brought a book with him that way he could pretend to bury his head in it and partially conceal his face. He wasn't sure if Hernandez would recognize him so Recker lifted the book up in front of his face, with his eyes just barely able to see over the edge of the book. It was enough to see what was going on, while at the same time, hoping he wouldn't be recognized.

It wasn't a particularly long meeting between Hernandez and Brinson. It seemed as though it was only a verbal type of meeting as Recker didn't observe anything being passed between them. One thing he did notice was Hernandez appeared to be doing most of the talking. And it didn't always seem that friendly as Hernandez talked somewhat animated at times to explain whatever his point was. After about fifteen minutes, they seemed to be done. Hernandez pushed his chair out and stood, giving a few last words to the banker, none of which appeared to be that pleasant either, judging from the veins popping out of the side of his neck.

"Hernandez is leaving," Recker said.

"I urge you to proceed with caution," Jones replied.

"Don't I always?"

"Do I really need to respond to that?"

Recker laughed, knowing how preposterous it sounded. "Gotta hurry before Brinson leaves."

"If you intend to do this, it might be better if you let him leave," Haley said.

"Why?"

"What if someone still has eyes on him?"

"That's a good point, Mike," Jones said, hoping that would persuade him not to meet him yet. "If he is not there of his own free will, they very well could be watching him. And if they see you sitting with him, who knows what would happen after that?"

"All right, you convinced me," Recker said.

"So, you'll come back here to the office?"

"No, I'll just follow Brinson as he leaves and pull him over somewhere."

"How did I know that's where this was headed?"

"Lucky guess?"

"Hardly."

A few minutes later, Brinson finally got up from his table and started walking along the street. Recker quickly paid for his meal and took off after him, staying far enough behind at first to see what the man was up to. As he walked, Recker kept looking all around to see if he could spot another tail on Brinson, but he didn't notice anything. After another ten minutes of walking, Recker finally sped up, ready to pull him to the side. Recker waited until they got to the right building until he finally caught up with him, wanting to make sure they went into a building where they could have some privacy to talk. Once they finally passed in front of the bookstore, Recker nudged Brinson to the side with his shoulder. Recker kept pushing him to the door with his body without much of a problem. When Brinson turned around to object to how he was being treated, Recker threw open the door and shoved him inside.

"What is going on?" Brinson asked.

Recker didn't answer and instead looked back toward

the street through the window. "You know if anybody's watching you?"

"Excuse me?"

"Anyone following you?"

"I'm not in the habit of being followed."

"Yeah, well, there's a first time for everything, isn't there?" Recker said.

"What is this all about?"

Recker looked around the bookstore and saw a couple of chairs by a shelf in the corner of the store. "That'll work well. Over there." He pointed.

"I'm not going anywhere until you tell me what this is all about."

Recker grabbed him by the arm and forcefully shoved him to the spot he wanted him to go. Luckily Brinson was not as big or as strong as Recker, so he wasn't able to put up much opposition to his demands. When they finally got to the corner, Recker pushed him toward one of the chairs.

"Here. Sit down."

"I'm not..."

Recker interrupted him before he could object. "I said sit," he forcefully said. "Then I'll tell you what this is all about."

Brinson took a deep breath, then figured he should comply with the man's wishes. Since he wasn't hurt yet, he could only assume the man didn't have intentions of harming him somehow. Especially in a bookstore. Brinson didn't know where he went wrong, but somewhere along the way, he figured he must have taken a wrong turn in his life. First dealing with Nowak and Hernandez, now with this guy in front of him, who he also assumed wanted him for some illegal or immoral reason. Brinson sat, waiting for the other shoe to drop, waiting for the man to tell him what he wanted, which was sure to be something he didn't want to do.

"Well?" Brinson asked.

"Well, what?"

"Well, what do you want? Let's get on with it."

"I'd like to know what you were doing with Gabriel Hernandez back there at the restaurant?" Recker asked.

"Having lunch. That's what most people do at a restaurant, right?"

"Most people. Except I noticed neither of you had any."

"Decided we weren't hungry," Brinson said.

"Listen, if you're in trouble, maybe I can help you. If you're knee deep in something you shouldn't be of your own accord, then maybe I can help soften the blow, so you don't get hurt as bad. Either way, it's your choice. But either way, you're gonna tell me what I wanna know."

"Why should I tell you anything?"

Recker reached inside his jacket and pulled out a wallet with a badge and ID card. "Detective Mike Scarborough."

Brinson got a weird look on his face. He looked both scared and relieved at the same time. Recker had trouble reading him. He couldn't be sure what Brinson was feeling at the moment.

"I really wanted to go to the police, but I just couldn't," Brinson said.

Recker was a little surprised he just blurted it out but was happy considering it saved them both a lot of time and aggravation of him trying to coerce the information out of him. "What's going on?"

"Couple weeks ago, I got a call out of the blue from some woman named Stephanie. She said she was interested in trying to raise some capital for a new business she was starting and asked for a meeting with me."

"And you did?"

"Yeah. Everything seemed fine. Met one or two times after that, then I learned what she was really after. She wanted me to falsify records and documents from some of my other clients and siphon the funds into an offshore account in her name."

"And you agreed?" Recker asked, sure there must have been more to the story.

"I had to. She..."

"She's got something on you, doesn't she?"

Brinson looked down and shamefully nodded. "Yes."

"What?"

"I had an indiscretion a couple weeks ago."

"What kind of indiscretion?" Recker asked.

"Look, I'm married. I have a beautiful wife, a son, a daughter, and I love them very much."

Recker closed his eyes and sighed, knowing full well where this was going. "And?"

"One night I stopped at the bar for some drinks with a couple buddies of mine. Towards the end when everyone started leaving, this woman approached me and started talking. At first, I didn't think much of it but after a while, and a few more drinks, she started really coming on to me, like really aggressive."

"And you couldn't say no?"

Brinson looked like he was fighting back tears as he shook his head, not able to say anything at first. "I swear I didn't want to, but she was just..."

"Yeah, I know, it was all her," Recker said, not really finding much sympathy for the man. Though he was reasonably sure Nowak had set the meeting up and planted the woman, it still took two to tango.

"I just... wasn't strong enough to say no."

"And you two went to some shady motel or something?"

"Yeah, something like that."

"Let me guess, a couple days after that meeting with this Stephanie woman, you started getting some compromising photos?" Recker said.

"How'd you know?"

"You're not the first sucker to fall for that trick."

"They said if I didn't help them they'd send the pictures to my wife and ruin me," Brinson replied. "She'd divorce me, take the kids, the house, everything. I couldn't let that happen."

"Ever think of just being honest and telling your wife everything that happened?"

Brinson just shrugged, not sure what else to say.

"Never know. She might've just surprised you and believed your story. Maybe she would've hung with you.

You know that whole marriage thing, for better or worse, in tough times and all that jazz."

"I didn't want to take chances."

"So, what have you done with them so far?" Recker asked.

"Well, not much really. I told them it would take some time for all that. If I rushed things and made mistakes, somebody would catch on fast."

"So, you haven't actually sent any money to them?"

"Not yet, no," Brinson answered. "That's what the meeting at the restaurant was about. He was upset it was taking this long and wanted me to hurry it up. Said if I hadn't sent the first payment through within the next five days, then my wife would get the first set of pictures."

Recker sat there for a minute, thinking of their next move.

"What do I do?" Brinson asked.

"You'll go back to your office and undo everything you've done so far."

"But the pictures."

"Unless you want a long prison sentence, that's exactly what you're gonna do. I'll take care of Hernandez and his boss."

"But, my wife?"

"I'll visit your wife and tell her someone's trying to blackmail you with fake pictures," Recker said. "I'll tell her you're cooperating with us and that as a result of that, someone may try to get back at you with photoshopped pictures. That should satisfy her."

Brinson took a huge sigh of relief. "Thank you."

"Don't thank me yet. You just make sure you undo anything."

"What do you want me to do after that?"

"Nothing. After that, you keep going on with your job like nothing else is happening."

"But Hernandez... he's gonna contact me again," Brinson said. "What am I gonna tell him?"

"You tell him it'll be a couple days. That should be enough time for us to get to work on them. I'll be in touch with you to see if there's any further contact."

"OK. Thank you. I really appreciate it."

Recker nodded at him as Brinson got up and left. Recker continued sitting there for a few minutes, trying to take everything in. He had the com on the whole time, so Jones and Haley could hear everything said.

"Well, what do you guys think?" Recker asked.

"I would say Nowak is going to give us problems," Haley replied.

Jones was silent for a moment, trying to collect his own thoughts. "I would tend to agree."

"I think we can all agree on one thing," Recker said. "If she sticks around, she's definitely gonna wind up giving us more problems than Vincent."

"I'm afraid you might be right about that."

"What do you wanna do now?" Haley asked.

"Right now, I'll go talk to Brinson's wife like I said I would. After that, I dunno. Try to stop this mess somehow."

"Might be a taller order than it seems."

"I know. I've also got a feeling it won't be so easy."

18

Recker had just finished talking to Mrs. Brinson and was walking back to his car, as he reached the door and was about to unlock it, he felt an object jam into the small of his back.

"I wouldn't reach for anything if I was you," a voice said. "In case you were wondering, I'm not using my finger."

Recker slowly raised his arms into the air. "I know the barrel of a gun when I feel it."

"Good. Do as you're told and maybe you'll live through this."

"Maybe?"

The man took a few steps back so Recker could turn around and face him. As he did, the man smiled at him. "Maybe not."

"Can I put my hands down now, Mr. Hernandez?"

"Just so you know, I don't have the only gun pointed at you, in case you had some funny ideas."

"I never have funny ideas," Recker said. "Cute ones sometimes, but never funny."

"Smart guy."

"Mildly intelligent."

"All right, you can cut the jokes now," Hernandez said. He then did a pat down on Recker and removed both his guns, sticking them in his own belt. "OK. You can put your arms down now."

Before doing so, Recker stuck his finger in his ear, pretending to scratch it. He was actually turning his com on to let the others know what was happening. Then he put his hands down and looked around to see who else was out there. He couldn't see anyone at first, but that didn't mean nobody was there. He could've tried to give Hernandez a problem right then and there but decided to let it play out and see where the situation was headed.

"Your boss know you're out here on the street playing with guns?" Recker asked.

"There you go with the jokes again."

"Want me to keep going?"

"No, I want you to shut your mouth."

A few seconds later, another car pulled up alongside them, ready to take them away. Recker resisted getting in at first. Hernandez pushed his gun further into Recker's back to give him some encouragement.

"I really shouldn't leave my car behind," Recker said.

"In."

"You do realize if my car's left here, eventually some-body's gonna come looking for it."

"So what? We'll be long gone by then. Get in."

Recker complied with the man's orders and got into the back seat, Hernandez sitting next to him, continuing to jab his gun into Recker's ribs. Just to make sure he didn't try anything funny, there was another man on the opposite side of Recker, along with a man in the front passenger seat.

"Looks like we got a full house in here," Recker said. "Where we heading?"

"You'll know when we get there," Hernandez replied.

"Well, can you at least tell me what this is about?"

"You know."

"I do? See that's the thing, I really don't. Maybe you could explain it to me?"

"You just had to go meddling into the Brinson thing, didn't you?" Hernandez asked.

"Well that's kind of my nature."

"I saw you talking to him in the bookstore. Considering you're now talking to his wife, we can only assume you somehow put the brakes on our deal."

"You know what they say about assuming."

"You know what they also say about meddling in someone else's business. It can get you killed."

"That a fact?"

"So is that where we're going?" Recker asked. "Dumping me in a river? Concrete slab? In a ditch?"

"Not just yet. Ms. Nowak would like to have another chat with you first."

"Oh, I look forward to it."

Once Recker had pushed his comm on, Jones and Haley had been listening to everything in the office. Their cars had tracking devices on them, in case of a situation where it wasn't known where they were so they could be located, which was why Recker was pushing to use his car. But it really didn't matter. Their com devices were also equipped with a GPS chip inside, so Jones was able to pull up his location on the computer. Now the only question was how to get him out.

"I'm gonna have to go," Haley said.

He was eager to get back out in the field. It'd been four weeks since he'd been shot in the leg and he was no longer on crutches. He actually felt pretty good. He was only walking with a slight limp at this point, hardly even noticeable. The biggest question was how he'd move if he got into a jam. If he had to twist, turn, and run, would his injury worsen? But Haley wasn't thinking about that now. His only concern was helping his friend out of a tough spot. Judging by Jones' lack of response, he could tell he wasn't that keen on the idea.

"There's no one else," Haley said.

"We could call Vincent."

"Malloy's still out of action. He's the only one in his bunch I know is tough enough to handle this. And with Vincent still looking to take Nowak out, he may say it's worth getting Mike caught in the crossfire if it means taking out the rest of her group at the same time."

Jones looked at him and nodded, reluctantly agreeing with his view. "I suppose that is true."

"Look, I know you don't wanna put me out there again before I'm ready... but I am. They said six weeks, and it's only been four, but I feel fine. I've been working out extra, I'm moving OK, there's nothing to hold me back. It's not like I'm going out there on crutches again. It's gotta be me."

Jones nodded again, knowing they didn't have much time to debate it. "You should get going. I'll let you know which way they go."

Haley rushed out the door and got into his car, driving towards Recker's last known position. As he was driving, Jones contacted him to tell him if the car that had Recker turned on a different street. Only a few minutes after Haley had left, the dot signifying Recker's position had stopped.

"Oh dear," Jones mumbled, knowing it was a bad sign they stopped already. He was hoping it wouldn't be for a little while to give Haley a chance to catch up to them. Jones hopped onto another computer to plug the coordinates in then called Haley to let him know.

"Chris, looks like Mike's now stationary."

"Where?" Haley asked.

"Address comes back to a factory on the outskirts of the city. I'm looking up now whether it's still in use."

"How far away?"

"You've probably got another twenty minutes or so to go."

"I'll step on it."

Hernandez had just gotten Recker out of the car and they approached the abandoned food factory. It had only recently gone out of business, with Nowak acquiring the property only two months ago.

"Oh, no thanks fellas, I'm pretty full. I ate earlier," Recker said.

"Let's go," Hernandez said, giving him a push in the back.

Recker and his four bodyguards went inside as they waited for Nowak to show up. Once inside, one of the men found a chair for Recker to sit in. Then they tied him to it with a rope.

"Not very hospitable of you guys," Recker said.

Hernandez sighed, getting tired of Recker's smart aleck mouth. He wanted this assignment to be done with. "Do you ever get tired of the jokes?"

"No, not really. Why? Do you?" Recker could tell he was getting on the man's nerves and only hoped he could keep it up. He figured the more annoyed he got, the less focused he would be when the time came to kill him, which would make it an easier task.

About five minutes passed before Nowak finally appeared, surrounded by three more of her men. Absent was Milton. Hernandez came over to the door to greet her before she got within range of Recker.

"He give you any trouble?" Nowak asked.

"None at all."

"Strange. What about his partner?"

"No sign of him," Hernandez answered.

Nowak instructed the three men she came in with to

wait outside, just in case Recker's partner showed up. She remembered what she was told from the hotel, about someone having a laser pointed at Milton, so she knew Recker had one. The fact he came so easily was another thing that alarmed her. Nowak then walked over to him, standing just in front of him.

"You look a little overdressed for a place like this," Recker said, observing her expensive-looking black dress. It looked like she was dressed for a gala or a fancy dinner party.

"I like to dress up for important people."

"Let me know when he gets here."

Nowak smiled. "You know it doesn't have to be like this."

"Like what?"

Nowak pointed at him. "Like this. You sitting in a chair tied up. Adversaries with me. Enemies."

"I hadn't thought of us as enemies."

"But you're stepping in between my business dealings, costing me money."

"Told you I would," Recker said. "You wanna do illegal stuff with other illegal people, that's on you and I really don't care. When you bring innocent people into things, that's when I get involved."

"I'd hardly call Mr. Brinson an innocent party."

"Oh, come on, hooking him up with a woman so he'd cheat on his wife and help you embezzle funds isn't exactly the same as comparing him to a thief or a murderer who does it because he enjoys it."

Nowak walked around Recker's chair, putting her

hand on his shoulder and running it across his back. "You know something? I really like you. I really do. I'm not sure what it is about you, but I find you have a magnetic personality that draws me closer to you."

"If only I had a dollar for every time I heard that."

"But there's one thing that really irritates me about you and it's that high moral compass you walk around with."

"I'm surprised there's only one."

"You see, you're already proving to be a pain."

"Not the first time I've heard that either," Recker said.

"And I can't have you going around, continuing to interfere in my business. Especially as I'm going up against Vincent."

"Is this where you and I part company?"

Nowak put her hand on his face and rubbed his cheek. "It doesn't have to be that way. Not if we come to an understanding."

"Such as?"

"Well, let's look at your options here. I will offer you a deal because I like you and I really value what you could bring to the table."

"Encouraging."

"Agree to help me, not interfere in my business again, and you can walk out of here with all your body parts still attached as God has given you."

"And if I don't agree?" Recker asked.

"Well, I'm afraid you're kind of a loose cannon. And as much as I like you, I can't afford to have you running around the city getting in my way again. So, as a consequence, you'd have to be buried here." Since Recker was tied up and couldn't reject her advances, Nowak sat on his lap then kissed him on the lips. "Or you could join me." Nowak then kissed him again, hoping to weaken his defenses and bring him to his senses.

Recker still wasn't the least bit interested in joining her but knew he had to do something quickly. Though he assumed somebody was coming, thanks to leaving his com on, he couldn't be sure when that help was arriving. The only thing he could do was stall.

"So, what's it gonna be?" Nowak asked.

Recker softened his stance, trying to make it seem like he was interested in her. "Doesn't seem like it's much of a choice, does it?"

"I don't think so."

"I guess my mind's made up then."

Nowak then planted another kiss on him, Recker pretending that he enjoyed this one. "I promise you won't regret it."

"So, what do we do first?" Recker asked.

"I have plans. We'll discuss them later."

Though Nowak was enjoying sitting on his lap, she finally got off him, though she couldn't resist touching him some more. She eventually was able to break her hand away from him and walked back over to Hernandez.

"Untie him," Nowak said.

Hernandez looked at Recker, not really sure about doing what he was told. He didn't trust him as much as his boss seemed to. "You sure that's a good idea?"

"Yes. He'll play ball with us."

"How can you be so sure?"

"He'll do what he's told."

"But what if he takes off after we leave here and we don't see him again?" Hernandez asked.

"We don't have to worry about that. Because he won't be on his own from here on out. We will always have a few people with him to make sure he complies with what we want."

"But we can't have someone with him twenty-four, seven, can we?"

Nowak smiled. "Why not? If he's not with you guys, then he'll be with me."

"OK, if you say so."

"Untie him and bring him to the new place," Nowak said, walking toward the door.

"Where are you going?"

"I have something else to deal with right now. Take him to the new place and wait until I get there."

"As you say."

Nowak left the building, taking with her the three men who she left waiting outside. Once she was gone, Hernandez went back over to Recker. He still didn't have a good feeling about untying him and letting him loose. He wasn't as confident as his boss he was going to join their team. Hernandez took a deep breath, then walked around the back of Recker and started cutting loose the rope. Recker stretched his arms around, then got up from the chair.

"Boss seems to put a lot of faith in you," Hernandez

said. "Me... not so much. You do anything other than what she tells you and I'll put a bullet in you myself."

"I'll remember that."

"See that you do."

Recker put his hand out, hoping to get what belonged to him. "Can I have my guns back now?"

Hernandez smiled and shook his head. "Not just yet. Not until we actually see you're upholding your end of things."

"Well how am I gonna do that if I don't have my stuff?"

"When the time comes."

Then, Recker heard Jones' voice in his ear. "Mike, Chris will be there momentarily." Recker tilted his head and moved it around so it wasn't obvious someone was in his ear. It was a good thing his com device was so small it wasn't noticeable unless someone really was looking for it.

"All right, let's go," Hernandez said, pointing to the door with his gun. Recker walked in front of everyone. Once he got to the door and opened it, he stopped. "Why are you stopping?"

"Sorry," Recker replied. "Habit. I never go through a door without knowing what's on the other side. Something I picked up over the years."

Hernandez wasn't impressed and didn't want to hear it. "Keep going."

Recker did as he was told and stepped outside, looking around to see if he could see Haley. He couldn't, but he sure hoped he was there. He was only a couple of feet from the car when another voice boomed in his ear.

"Hernandez is to your left," Haley said. "You take him, I'll take out the others. I'll shoot on your move."

Seeing as how he was almost at the car, Recker wasted no time in following Haley's directions. Almost immediately, he twirled around and rushed Hernandez, spearing him in the gut with his shoulder, knocking them both to the ground. The blow from Recker knocked the gun from Hernandez' hand. As they wrestled on the ground, the other three removed their guns to help their teammate. Haley was on a rooftop on the building directly facing the food factory entrance. As soon as the other three removed their guns, Haley opened fire with his sniper rifle. Within the span of a few seconds, he had successfully taken out the other three men without much of a struggle. The men didn't know where the shots were coming from and didn't have a chance to make it back inside the building for cover.

After a couple minutes of wrestling, Recker got the upper hand after delivering a few punches to the side of Hernandez' face. Recker reached for the gun lying on the ground and grabbed hold of it. Just as he did, Hernandez hurriedly removed one of his other guns to try to stop Recker's progress. Recker quickly spun around on the ground and fired three shots rapidly in succession, all of which lodged into Hernandez' midsection. The man instantly dropped to his knees, then face down on the ground as the blood he was losing quickly soaked the rest of his body, as well as the concrete underneath him.

Recker got up and checked each of the men to see if any were still breathing, though none of them were. He then looked for Haley but didn't see where he was. A few seconds later, he noticed Haley's car zooming in. Recker quickly hopped in as they sped out of the area.

"A little close for comfort," Recker said.

Haley smiled. "Had it all the way. Where to?"

"Let's head to that hotel Nowak's staying."

"Why?"

"Because I don't like her."

"Fair enough."

Recker let Jones know he was OK and where they were heading. Though Jones objected to their destination, Recker didn't pay much mind to him and went, anyway. When they got to the hotel, they cautiously moved through it, not sure if Nowak's men would be waiting for them. Recker thought it unlikely since he didn't think word would get back to her so soon, but he couldn't say for sure. They eschewed the elevator and went up the stairs.

"What's the plan?" Haley asked, trying to keep up with his partner, though he was falling a little behind due to his leg.

"Shoot whoever gets in our way."

"Oh. Good plan."

"You all right?" Recker asked.

"A little sore. No big deal."

"I can take care of it on my own."

"Don't worry about it. I'm fine. Do it like last time?"

"No, I think they're on to that trick by now. Let's just rush them."

Once they finally got to Nowak's floor, they could

immediately tell something was different. They looked toward her room and didn't see the guards. That was a red flag right away. She wouldn't have left herself unprotected like that.

"Maybe they're all inside having a powwow," Haley said.

"I kind of doubt it."

The two men hurried over to the door. Recker took a quick jiggle of the handle to see if it was open, but it was locked. Recker then bent down to pick the lock as Haley stood guard and watched for any unwelcome visitors passing by. After a minute, Recker had the door unlocked. He slowly opened it as the two men stepped inside. Once in, they split off to check the room. But there was no one there. After a few minutes, the two met back up in the main room.

"Empty," Haley said.

Recker sighed, wishing Nowak was there. If she was, he could've ended her entire organization then and there. Now, they'd probably have to start over.

They stayed a few minutes to search the drawers, cabinets, and closets to see if any information had been left behind, but there was nothing of value. They let Jones know their findings then went straight back to the office. Jones was already hard at work trying to find out Nowak's new location when the boys got back there.

"Anything?" Recker asked.

Jones voiced a loud sigh, which was all the response that Recker needed. "I'm afraid not."

"She just up and vanished?"

"She checked out of her room yesterday."

"And you can't get a fix on her now?"

"Unfortunately, not," Jones answered. "Everything I used to track her before has been no help. Phone, cards, everything's been silent the last few days."

"Most likely she's switched everything," Haley said.

"Undoubtedly so."

"Damn," Recker said. "If she had stayed one more day, we could've ended things." He was more than a little disappointed in the developments, as he knew that meant Nowak would be around a lot longer, since she'd now have some time to regroup. He viewed Nowak as a much more dangerous threat than Vincent as she didn't seem like she was as interested as Vincent was in having a business arrangement that benefited both of them. She was only out for herself.

"The only thing we can do right now is put her to the side and work on other things," Jones said. "At some point I'm sure she'll turn up and we'll run into her again."

"Sooner rather than later, probably."

"Yes, well, in the meantime, we can start working again on our own things."

Recker then looked at Haley. "Assuming you're well enough to keep things going for a week, you can do it without me, if that's all right."

"Works for me," Haley said.

"Why?" Jones asked. "Where do you intend on going?"

"You forget that Mia thing?"

"Oh yes. I had forgotten for a moment."

"She hasn't."

"You'd like to go now?"

"No time like the present," Recker answered.

"Well, since it's relatively slow at the moment, I see no harm in it," Jones said.

"Good, because I never thought I'd say this."

"What?"

"I think I need a vacation."

CLOSE RANGE PREVIEW

Enjoy the following 3 chapter preview of the next book in The Silencer Series, Close Range.

19

Recker had just gotten back from his week-long vacation; him and Mia visiting the Jersey shore for seven days. They'd had a great time, and Recker felt like a normal person again, without having to worry about death and danger lurking around every corner. Mia would have been fine if they never actually made it back to the city, but as much of a good time as Recker was having, he was getting the itch to come back. Going on vacation was a nice change of pace, especially being alone with Mia for the week, but there was only so much inactivity that Recker could stand without beginning to go crazy. He was ready for the vacation to end when it did.

They got back to Philadelphia, and Recker was ready to get back to work right away. Unfortunately for him, for whatever reason, there seemed to be a bit of a lull in the action. There was nothing for him to do. He stayed at home for two days before going back to the office, feeling like he had to do something besides just sitting around all day. When Recker walked into the office, it looked the same as it always did, not that he was really expecting anything different, but being away for a week, he realized he missed the place. Jones and Haley had their backs to him, plugging away at their respective computers. Once they heard the door shut, they stopped typing and spun around, smiling at their partner, happy to see their friend again.

"There he is," Haley said, getting up and walking over to him, slapping hands, and giving him a bro-hug. "Good to have you back, man."

Recker smiled. "Good to be back."

"Michael, you look refreshed," Jones said.

"I feel good."

"Looks like you even got a little bit of a tan," Haley said, observing his darker complexion.

"Mia liked to hit the beach."

"Thought maybe you'd like being away so much you'd forget to come back."

"Not likely."

"You have a good time?"

"Uh, yeah, yeah, I guess I did. Better than I assumed I would. It's been a while since I've taken that kind of time off."

"If anyone deserved it, it was you," Jones said.

"I don't think I've ever seen you looking this relaxed," Haley said. "You look so stress-free right now."

"Spending a week at the beach with your beautiful girlfriend I'm sure helps."

Recker smirked. "I'm sure it does."

"As a matter of fact, he's almost looking too relaxed."

"Don't start, David."

"No, I'm just saying... it's something about your face. It's almost like it's glowing or something."

"Isn't that what they say about women who are expecting?" Haley asked.

"It is. I hope that's not what's happening here. I'm surprised he can stand up as well as he is right now. I half expected his legs to be wobbly after all the..."

"OK," Recker said, slightly amused by the teasing. "Can we get off my love life now and get back to work?"

"I think your love life is more interesting," Haley said with a laugh. "So, what exactly did you two do the entire time?"

Jones put his finger in the air. "Don't ask questions you may not want the answer to, Chris."

Recker stood still, though he moved his jaw from side to side as he looked at his two friends, wondering when they were going to be done with their kidding. It kept up for several more minutes, both men seeming to be beyond happy at teasing him.

"Are you done yet?" Recker asked.

"No, not quite," Jones answered. "I'm actually surprised you have much of a tan at all. You know, Chris and I had figured you two would spend the whole week shuttered in your hotel room."

"Well, I figured you would come out at least one day," Haley said. "I mean, unless you just went to a tanning bed." Haley then snapped his fingers and pointed at Jones.

"You know, I bet that's what happened. He didn't want us to think he just played inside all day, so the day before he came home, he just went to one of those tanning salons to make us think he was outside all the time."

Recker folded his arms and kept a straight face, doing his best not to laugh. Though he wouldn't have minded if the teasing had ended, he couldn't deny it was mildly entertaining. And his friends kept up their assault, throwing around more jokes and funny insults in the next few minutes than they had in the previous month. Eventually, after what seemed like forever, though it was probably not more than ten minutes or so, the joking died down. After a minute of quiet, Recker assumed it was over.

"Oh, are we done now?" Recker asked.

Jones and Haley looked at each other.

"Yeah, I think I'm done," Haley said.

"Yes, I am as well," Jones replied.

"Oh good. Maybe now we can get back to work?" Recker said.

"Well, that would be a good idea if there was any work to get back to."

"What?"

"Why do you think we took the time to kid you as long as we did?" Jones asked. "It's because we have nothing on the agenda."

"No work?"

"None whatsoever. Apparently, when you went on vacation, the criminals of this city did as well."

"You guys haven't had any action?" Recker asked.

"One or two minor things. Nothing major."

"Vincent and Nowak?"

"Completely silent between the two of them."

"Oh," Recker said, looking slightly disappointed. "Well, I guess that's good."

Jones could see the disappointment on his face. "It's the general idea of our operation, is it not? To get rid of crime as much as possible to the point where we're no longer needed. That is the goal, right?"

"Uh, yeah, yeah, I guess it is. Still would be nice to be busy, though."

"I'm sure something will come along soon enough."

"Why, are you keeping tabs on something?"

"Not at the moment, no."

"Oh. You sounded like you thought something was coming."

"Merely a figure of speech," Jones said. "I highly doubt the criminal activity has come to a screeching halt for good. I'm sure it's just a matter of time until you're back in the saddle and shooting up the saloon again."

"So, if there's nothing to do, then what are you guys doing?"

"I didn't say there's nothing to do. I said there are no imminent threats. I'm doing the same thing I'm always doing. Keeping my eyes open and monitoring things."

"So, uh, what do you want me to do?" Recker asked.

"At the moment... nothing."

"There's nothing for me to do?"

"That's right."

"So, what am I supposed to do?"

"If I were you, I'd go home and spend a few more days with your better half. I'm sure she'd love to have you home for another day or two."

"She went back to work again today too."

"Well then, go home and take a nap," Jones said.

"Do you realize what you're asking me to do?"

A small smirk emerged on Jones' face, though he was doing his best to hide it and not make fun of Recker's plight. Jones knew asking a man like him to do nothing was a very difficult task.

"I've spent the last ten years living in almost constant danger," Recker said. "Then I go on vacation, I come back, and there's still nothing for me to do."

"It's burning a hole through you right now, isn't it?"

"Getting close."

"You just have the overwhelming urge to go out there and shoot somebody, don't you?"

Recker put his index finger in the air and then bent it several times in rapid succession. "It hasn't been used in a while."

"Well, for the moment, you're just going to have to exercise it in other ways."

Recker and Jones looked at each other, both realizing how weird that sounded. Jones just waved at him, each knowing that's not how it was intended to sound.

"Mike, go home, relax, put your feet up, watch TV, read a book, go to a museum, I'm sure everything will be back to its usual hectic self in a few days. You've earned the extra time off. Take it."

Recker sighed, not really wanting extra time off. Seven

days was more than enough for him. But as things were, there was nothing else he could do. Haley was basically in the same position, though he didn't mind not being busy. It was almost like a vacation for him too. But not having anyone in his life to spend the time with like Recker did, he just spent it in the office, monitoring things along with Jones.

"All right, well, I guess I'll go home then," Recker finally said. "If something happens, you know where to reach me."

"You'll be the first one I call," Jones replied.

"Should I report back in the morning tomorrow?"

"Let's just play it by ear. If you're needed, I'll call you. If you don't hear from me, just assume there's still nothing going on and take another day off."

"Wonderful."

Recker went back to his apartment, and with Mia still at work, soon found himself bored. Most of his life revolved around work or her, and with neither of them available right then, just kind of sputtered around. He put the TV on for a bit, but daytime TV just wasn't for him.

"How do people watch this stuff?"

He turned the TV off and went on his laptop for a bit, looking at the news section, secretly hoping he could find some sort of trouble he could interject himself into. After an hour or two of surfing the internet, and not finding anything to his liking, he turned that off as well. Recker went to the window and stared out at the parking lot. He got bored after a minute or two. He then went back to the TV and put on a baseball game which was played the night before. Since he had the baseball subscription package that let him watch any game from around the league, he spent the entire day watching baseball games. It was the only thing that didn't bore him or make him restless.

Recker wound up watching four different games in a row. He had completely lost track of time and didn't even realize Mia was already on her way home. It was a little after six o'clock and she was done her shift. Recker didn't even hear the keys rattling in the lock of the door. It wasn't until the door opened that his eyes left the baseball game on TV and saw his girlfriend entering their apartment. He quickly got up and walked over to her.

"Hey," Mia said with a smile, happy to see him. "What are you doing here?"

"Uh, I live here."

Mia laughed, then gave him a kiss. "Yes, I know that. I didn't think you'd be here though."

"Why not?"

"Well, because you've been gone for a week, so I figured you'd be swamped with work stuff."

"Oh. Well, would you believe there's not a thing to do right now?"

"Really?" Mia seemed as surprised as he was at the lack of action available.

"I guess since I went on vacation all the bad guys figured they'd wait until I got back to do something again."

Mia put her hands on his face and kissed him some more. "Well, I guess they haven't heard you're back yet."

"I suppose."

"Don't act so disappointed."

"I'm just... I'm not used to not doing anything."

"And it's killing you, isn't it?"

"A little bit."

"Don't worry," Mia said. "I'm sure it's just one of those weird coincidences. I'm sure, much to my detriment, people will be back to shooting at you in the next few days. I'm sure you'd enjoy that, wouldn't you?"

"Not so much."

"So, what have you been doing all day?"

"Uh, not much. Just watching baseball."

"You've been doing that all day?"

"Yeah, everything else bored me to death," Recker said.

"Well, I think I can think of something that might not be so boring."

Recker smiled and picked her up. "So can I."

20

The next two weeks went by and the lack of action for the team continued. They'd never seen a stretch like this where they were so inactive. It was kind of bittersweet. Though they were obviously happy for the reduction in crime, they were used to being busy, and not having anywhere specific to go was something new they were having trouble adjusting to.

Recker had just arrived at the hospital after getting a message from Mia about meeting her there for lunch. He went into the cafeteria, and after not seeing his lovely girlfriend yet, found their usual table empty and took a seat. He sent her a text message to let her know he was there and got a reply a minute later to say she was on her way down. Once she got there, her and Recker grabbed a couple of trays to get some food, then sat back down. As they began eating, Recker noticed an unusual look about

Mia today. She seemed a little nervous or frazzled, not like her usual upbeat self.

"You OK?" Recker asked.

"Yeah, why?"

"Just seem... different."

"Different how?" Mia asked in a worried sounding voice.

"Like you're nervous or something."

"Oh. No. I'm not nervous. Why would I be?"

Recker grinned. "I don't know. That's why I asked."

"I'm fine."

Nothing about her answers sounded fine to Recker. Her voice was slightly cracking, the way it does when someone isn't confident in their answers and is trying to hide something. Her voice was giving it away though. Still, while Recker knew she was holding something back, he wasn't going to keep pressing her on it right then. He didn't like it when people did it to him, so he'd give the same courtesy he liked to get. Plus, he figured Mia would tell him when she was good and ready. Maybe it was a stressful day at work and she just needed to unwind a little bit.

"Tough day?" Recker asked.

"Umm, no, not particularly." Recker nodded, ready to drop the subject entirely. Knowing she was probably sounding weird, Mia made a concerted effort to sound more normal. "So, uh, still not much going on for you guys, huh?"

"No, not much. Maybe it's like the Old West. We came

in, cleaned up the town, and maybe now we gotta move on to another one and do the same thing."

Mia smiled, though it was clear she still had something else on her mind. It was a plastered-on smile that she had to manufacture to try to seem like she was interested. She could feel her heart racing as she thought about what it was she wanted to tell him. As they continued to eat, Recker looked down at Mia's hands, which appeared to be shaking as she took a bite of her food.

"Are you sure you're OK?" Recker asked.

"I'm fine. Why do you keep asking?"

"For one, your hands are shaking." Mia looked down at them and saw them trembling a little. "Two, you just don't seem like yourself."

"I don't?"

"Is there something wrong?"

Mia took a deep sigh to try to help her calm down and get out the words she wanted to say. But they just weren't coming. This was a life-altering statement about to come out of her mouth and she didn't know how to begin. She'd been thinking about it for several days, trying to think of the right way, the right environment, the right situation, but nothing ever seemed right. Every time she thought she was going to say something at the apartment, every time she tried to get the words out, she couldn't seem to force them out.

Recker was starting to get a little more concerned about her, seeing a few beads of sweat form on Mia's forehead. He couldn't imagine what was so tough she was struggling to deal with. He reached across the table and grabbed hold of Mia's hand, rubbing it to try to calm her down. Though he couldn't imagine what it might have been, it obviously had to be big for her to be acting this way.

"Just calm down," Recker said. "Relax."

Mia took a gulp and nodded. "OK."

"Everything's OK."

She could feel her heart rate come down a little bit, though it still felt like it was racing pretty good. She took a few more deep breaths to help.

"Now what's going on?" Recker asked.

"Umm, I just... I don't quite know how to say this."

Those were strange words for Recker to hear, as she never really had a problem with talking to him before. He sat up a little straighter and released her hand as he tried to brace himself for what he assumed was a bombshell to come out of her mouth.

"I... um..."

Recker cleared his throat, wondering how long this was going to continue. He figured he was going to have to try to help her out by guessing at what the issue was. And he didn't like what he was thinking. But still, it seemed like a good possibility.

"Do you wanna break up?" Recker asked, figuring that was the issue. "Go our separate ways? Is that it?"

A surprised look came over Mia's face, mad at herself for giving off that impression. "No! No." She then switched seats so she could sit next to her boyfriend instead of across from him. She grabbed his hand again and smiled at him. "No, I love you. More than ever. Why would you think that?"

"Because you're sitting there looking nervous and you're having trouble talking about something. Figured maybe you wanted to find someone else or something."

"Of course not. You're stuck with me for life." Mia then leaned over and kissed him. "Unless that's what you want."

"What?"

"Is that what you want? To split up?"

Recker rolled his eyes. "No, it's not. My life has never been more complete since you've been in it. I just don't know what you're having a hard time with. Whatever the problem is, let me help."

Mia forced another smile. "I'm trying."

"I mean, is it work-related, something to do with us, something personal, what?"

"I just don't want anything to change with us."

"So, it's us?"

"I don't know how you're gonna react to this."

Now Recker was starting to get worried himself. He couldn't figure out what could have been troubling her so much.

"Mia, I can't help you if you don't tell me what's wrong." A few tears started to show in the corners of her eyes as she dabbed at them. "Whatever it is, we can get through it. But I have to know what the problem is first."

"It's not really a problem. It's just... things would change between us. And I don't know if you would still want to stick around."

Recker scrunched his eyebrows together as he tried to figure out what she was talking about. Mia took a few more deep breaths, determined to finally get the words out of her system. She squeezed Recker's hand a little tighter.

"Mike, I'm late."

"Late? Late for what?" Recker asked, assuming she just wanted to go back to work to avoid talking about it. "You just got here. It can't be time to go back already."

Mia shook her head. "No, I don't mean that. I mean... I'm late."

"Late?"

Mia nodded, hoping he'd get the message. Judging by his face, it didn't seem like he did though.

"What do you mean, you're late?"

Mia leaned back and put her hand on her stomach. "I'm late."

Recker sat there with his mouth open, stunned. He finally got the message. Maybe he knew all along and was just hoping she'd say something else instead of what he was thinking. In any case, there was no doubt about her meaning now. Mia sat there, trying to get a read on her boyfriend's face, hoping he was OK with the news. They'd never really discussed having kids before, so she wasn't sure how he was going to take it. Judging by the fact he wasn't jumping up and down, smiling and dancing, he didn't seem thrilled by the news.

"You're pregnant?"

Mia nodded. "Yeah."

"Are you sure?"

"Pretty sure."

"Well, I mean, just because you're late doesn't necessarily mean you're pregnant, right? Could be any number of things. Could just be stress."

Mia shook her head. "No, Mike. I took a test this morning. It said positive."

"Oh."

They sat there looking at each other for a minute, neither saying a word, trying to get their thoughts and feelings in perspective. The minute felt like an hour though. Recker wasn't sure what to say. Though Mia was happy with the news, that happiness was offset a little bit by not knowing what it meant for her and Recker's future together. She knew having a child was probably never in his plans. She just had to hope he still wanted to be there and could come to grips with being a father.

"So, what do you think?" Mia asked, somewhat fearful of the response.

This time it was Recker taking the deep breath. "I don't know. It's a lot to take in."

"Are you mad?"

Recker shook his head. "No, of course not. How could I be mad?"

"Well, I know this isn't probably something you saw coming or were ever hoping for."

"Uh, well, no, it wasn't."

"So, what are you thinking right now?"

Recker half-smiled and let out what could probably pass for a laugh, not even sure what he was thinking. It felt like his mind was swirling around in a thousand different directions.

"I don't really know. Are you planning on keeping it?"

"Yes," Mia answered. "I couldn't not do that. I mean, I would never judge someone else or force my beliefs on someone else, but for me, I couldn't give it up. It was our choice to be intimate and we have to live with the consequences and be responsible for it."

Recker nodded, understanding her point. "I agree with you."

"I guess the bigger issue is whether you're going to stick around for it."

"You think I would just leave you because of this?"

"I don't know. I guess I've been worried about it. I guess it's why I had such a tough time talking about it. Because I know it's not something you've ever really wanted, and I know it probably doesn't fit in with your work and all, so I don't know. I would hope not. I still love you and that wouldn't change. I would hope you felt the same way."

"I do. Nothing would change how I feel about you. I would think you'd know that."

"But this is different. This would be a huge change. For both of us. I don't know if anyone's ever really ready to be a parent, but for some people it's more of a change than others."

"Have you ever known me to run away from anything?"

"No."

"This isn't any different." Recker took another deep

breath. "I can't say this is something I've ever given a lot of thought to, or ever wished for, but I won't hide from it. I'll be there for you and the child. It may take some getting used to for me, and I may have to make some changes, but I'll be there."

Mia finally let out a real smile and gave her boyfriend a passionate kiss on the lips. "I'm so happy to hear you say that."

"You really thought I'd walk out on you because of this?"

"Uh, no, not really. It's just... it's a big change. And not everyone reacts to news like this the way you think they will. I guess I was just hoping you wouldn't pull a Mr. Hyde and change who you are after hearing it."

"I would never do that. Like I said, it might take some time to get used to being a father, and I may not always know the right thing to do, but I'll do my best."

"That's all I can ask. Well, almost all."

"What do you mean, almost all?"

"Uh," Mia said, faking a cough as she tried to figure out the best way to say the next piece of news. This part had to come second, as if Recker had decided to leave, it wouldn't have mattered, anyway. But now he was committed, it had to be asked.

"What is it, twins or triplets or something?"

Mia laughed. "Of course not. At least I don't think so. We wouldn't know right now, anyway."

"Mia, I doubt anything else could be as surprising as what you just said, so just spit it out."

"OK. I know you're committed to your work, and that's

fine, and I've always said I wasn't going to pressure you to do something else or anything."

"I feel a but coming on here."

"But, if we welcome a child into this world, do you really think it's best if you're still out there doing what you do?" Recker just looked at her for a few seconds, not sure how to respond. She could already feel the arguments coming on. "I know, I know. I'm not asking you to stop today or anything. All I'm saying is, I don't think it's a great idea to have a child who's always going to wonder if his father's coming home that day."

Recker looked away for a second and sighed, not believing they were having this conversation. "If the child doesn't know what I'm doing, he won't have to wonder."

"And if you come home shot? Or with blood? Or a broken bone? Or bruises? What do we tell them then?"

"That I do security work. It's the standard cover answer."

"Mike, that will only work for so long. I mean, you do dangerous things, you put yourself in dangerous spots and situations, not to mention you're still technically wanted by the police, you interact with criminals and crime lords... there's a very real possibility that if you keep doing that for the next ten or twenty years, eventually, one night you're not going to come home. Would you really want our child to grow up without a father?"

Recker stared at her, letting her words sink in. He knew she was right. But knowing she was right about walking away, and walking away, were two different things. This was the life he'd known for so long, he couldn't imagine doing anything else. And there was no debating her point of view. It was one he long held himself. A person in his position could only interact with the type of people he did before it eventually caught up to him. It was just a matter of time. But that was a decision he had long ago accepted. Bringing a child into the world would have to change that for him. At least that's what Mia hoped.

Mia knew it was hard for him to just walk away. It was so ingrained in him, that even fathoming any other career was an extremely difficult proposition. And she was sensitive to that. At least as much as any loving girlfriend could be. She never wanted to be someone who pushed their other half to do something they didn't want, or away from something they were good at, even if it was dangerous. And she still wasn't. She wanted it to be Recker's call to walk away on his own. He needed to be the one who called it quits because it was what he thought was the right decision, not because it was what Mia wanted. She knew that if he only quit because of her, he'd likely never be happy.

"Listen, I'm not asking you to quit today, or even tomorrow, or even this year. I just want you to start thinking about the possibility of maybe walking away at some point."

The strain on Recker's face was obvious as he struggled to reel everything in. After a minute, he started nodding. "I never really planned on making it to social security age or anything. I never was able to picture myself growing old and gray."

"I'm not gonna pressure you or anything, you know I'm not like that. I've never done that, and I never will. But it's not just about you anymore. It's about us. We're gonna have a family."

"I realize that. And, uh, I can't disagree with anything you're saying."

"Now I feel a but coming."

"It's gonna be hard for me to walk away."

"I know that. And I'm not saying you must do it now. I know you're not ready for that. And I don't want you to do something you're not ready to commit to yet. I just want you to start thinking about it. To start planning for the day in a year, or two years, or three years, when you eventually do walk away. That way David and Chris can start preparing for life without you."

"Life without me. Sounds funny to hear it."

"Do you think they'd have a problem if you eventually do that?"

"No, I don't think so. I dunno. When we started this, I don't know if David pictured it lasting forever."

"What did you think?"

"I wasn't really focused on the long term at that point. I'd just gotten back from London, needed a purpose, needed a way to find Agent Seventeen, needed to put my past behind me. That's pretty much all I was focused on at the time. A few years down the line... I wasn't even sure I'd make it that far."

"David could always find another person to replace you, couldn't he?"

"I'm sure he could. I'm sure I'm not the only one who

fits the profile. Chris proves that."

"So, you'll think about it?"

"What else would I do?" Recker asked. "I couldn't just sit home all day playing Mr. Mom. I need to be productive."

"Well, I wouldn't ask you to sit home all day. But there's things you could do."

"Like what?"

"You could start your own business. Money's not an issue."

"Doing what?"

"I don't know," Mia replied. "You could start your own security company. Or a consulting company, or even a private detective agency, you know, just a little more legal than what you do now."

"If I'm doing things similar to what I'm already doing, then what's the point?"

"The point would be that you're not the one who's actually out there getting shot at. Start a consulting business, you can advise others how to have better security. You can hire others to go out there while you sit in the office counting the money."

"Sitting in an office all day isn't exactly my cup of tea."

"I know it isn't. But we all must make changes to our life at some point, don't we? If not for ourselves, then for others."

Recker sighed again. "I'll start thinking about it."

Mia gave him a look suggesting she didn't quite believe him. That maybe he was just saying it to make her feel better or to shut her up. "Really?"

"No, I will. I promise. I know you're probably right, and at some point, for the sake of our family, I'll have to start making changes. I don't know, and can't promise, when that will be, but I will start thinking about it. And I know at some point, I'll have to walk away. I know that."

Mia smiled at him, knowing it was hard for him to admit that, or even say it. She was proud of him for not being stubborn about it and pulling away. She put her hand on his face and gave him a kiss.

"That's all I can ask. I love you."

"I love you too."

A few more minutes went by before Mia had to go back to work. As Recker watched her walk out of the cafeteria, his mind was suddenly hit with everything they just talked about. He let out several deep breaths, certainly not anticipating hearing anything close to the bombshells that had been told to him that day. This wasn't how he thought the day would go.

Now he started thinking about whether he should tell Jones and Haley or just keep it to himself for a while. He knew that whenever it was time to go, he wasn't just going to spring it on his partners suddenly. He'd want to give them plenty of time to prepare, and potentially find someone else if that's what they wanted. He tried to take his mind off his current issues by thinking of something else. He would have preferred to be in the middle of a gunfight right now. Anything but what he now had to deal with. But he couldn't. The situation was what it was and now he had to deal with it. He knew at some point, he would have to walk away. But not just yet.

21

After leaving the hospital, Recker checked in with Jones again to make sure there were no problems on the horizon. With the coast clear, and being told he wasn't needed, Recker went home to try to wrap his head around everything. Once he got there, he didn't do anything but plop himself down on the couch. He didn't turn the TV on, didn't try to keep himself busy, didn't do anything. Nothing except let his eyes focus on different objects around his apartment as he thought. He was going to be a father. There was nothing in the world that could have prepared him for those words.

Recker continued to think about everything Mia said to him. It was almost like she was there again. He pictured her sitting across from him, reliving the conversation over again, not forgetting a single word either of them said. He had never really pictured this day coming. He never had any thoughts or feelings about being a father. It would take some time to get used to. But now the day was here, he had to really think about his chosen profession. Mia was right. He couldn't continue what he was doing and have a family. It wouldn't be fair to them. To wait, to wonder, and to worry, every night, not sure if he would make it home that evening. As much as he wasn't ready to walk away from the job now, he knew he had to start giving it more thought. It was a reality. At some point, he was going to have to do it.

For the next hour, Recker thought about everything he'd been through in his life. All the tough and dangerous times. As scary as it was sometimes, it was difficult to imagine not going through it anymore. On the flip side, he imagined what his life would be like in the future. He pictured himself feeding bottles, changing diapers, cleaning up after a messy child, car seats, high chairs, pacifiers, play dates, school drop-offs, teacher conferences... the list just went on and on and on. Those images were more terrifying to him than facing off against the bad guys. His mind had trouble processing it all.

Luckily for him, his disturbing thoughts were interrupted by the sound of his phone ringing. He picked it up, hoping it was Jones, presenting him with a new case. Something to take his mind off his current situation. Strangely, it wasn't. It was a number he didn't initially recognize. Still, there was something familiar about it. The area code was one he knew. He hesitated in answering, but eventually decided to see who it was.

"Hello?"

"Hi. Wasn't sure you'd pick up or not."

Recker immediately recognized the female voice, though he was surprised she was calling. He was silent for a minute, making the caller think maybe he didn't remember who she was.

"You remember me, right?"

"I do. Michelle Lawson."

"It's been a while."

"It has."

"I guess you're wondering why I'm calling, huh?"

"I figured you'd get around to it at some point."

"I'd like to talk to you."

"Isn't that what we're doing now?" Recker asked.

"In person. You know how reliable phones are. Especially with your partner."

"You wanna meet?"

"Yes. The quicker the better."

"Is my number up?"

Lawson let out a laugh. "No, you're not in any danger. There's a situation that's come up that I'd like to go over with you. Not over the phone though."

"You're not setting me up?"

"You think I'd do that to you?"

"Maybe with some prodding from some old crusty superior who was forcing you to."

"Well, it's not. I give you my word everything's on the up and up. Besides, if it was the case, we could've taken you out when you were at the hospital a couple hours ago. Or at your apartment now."

Recker laughed, not believing he was so sloppy as to allow himself to get tailed. "You're following me."

"Uh, not exactly, no. We had a man at the hospital all day on the lookout for you, and another guy waiting by your apartment. So, we weren't exactly following you, we just knew eventually you would be at those places. We wanted to be there when you were. So, if the intention was to take you out, we wouldn't be having this conversation already."

"Unless I took out your guys first."

Recker could hear her smiling into the phone. "Somehow I wouldn't doubt that," Lawson said. "I wouldn't be asking you this unless it was extremely urgent. We really need to talk."

"OK. When and where?"

"Can you make it now?"

"Guess it depends on where it is."

"Let's make it one hour. I'll text you the address."

"OK. I'll be there."

"And don't bring your friends."

"Now you're sounding ominous," Recker said.

"Please, just trust me."

"OK."

After getting off the phone, Recker just stared at it for a minute, wondering what the big emergency was. He assumed she was telling the truth, and the plan wasn't to kill him, as it was unlikely they would contact him first, unless they were trying to lull him to sleep first to avoid more casualties. But he didn't really think that was it. Not that he trusted anyone in the CIA completely, Lawson genuinely seemed like someone who didn't stoop to using such tricks.

A few seconds later, he got the text message with the address. Before leaving, he looked it up on the computer. It was a vacant property in the King of Prussia area, not too far from the mall. It looked like it used to be an office building used by a doctor or a dentist. Recker thought about letting Jones know, that way he could track him, just in case things somehow went sideways. But there was no way Jones would sign off on the meeting without Recker telling him about it or having him bring Haley along. On the off chance it was a trap, he didn't want to risk Haley getting caught up in it. If it was a ruse, Recker knew the CIA would be bringing more people than he could probably count. Bringing Haley along wouldn't have changed the outcome.

After deciding to keep the meeting a secret, Recker got in his car and drove up the turnpike to the King of Prussia area. It was roughly a forty-five-minute drive until he got to the meeting place. Once he pulled into the parking lot, he observed three other black SUV's already parked. Recker made sure he didn't park too close to them, just in case he needed to get away quickly. Once he got out of the car, he noticed the SUV's were empty. He walked along the concrete sidewalk until he arrived at the front door, which surprisingly didn't have any guards there. He put his hand on his gun in case he had to draw it quickly.

As Recker got closer to the front door, a man in a suit with a shaved head and sunglasses suddenly appeared beyond the glass door. Recker stopped in his tracks as he waited for the man to make a move. The man, who was obviously with the agency, opened the door and stood to the side of it, looking like a doorman as he held it open, waiting for Recker to approach. Recker continued walking toward it, and once he got there, the agent pointed to his right, indicating the spot to where he was supposed to go.

Recker went inside, immediately seeing Lawson sitting in what used to be a waiting room. It was still carpeted and had furniture, including some chairs and a few tables. Everything looked new though.

"Have a seat," Lawson said. She then looked to the agent. "That'll be all, thank you."

Recker turned around and watched the agent go, leaving only him and Lawson in the room. At least as far as he could tell. There were some other doors which probably used to be offices or exam rooms, which could have housed the other agents Recker knew were in the area.

"Like what you've done with the place," Recker said. "Carpet looks new."

"It was recently acquired."

"Where's everyone else?"

"What? Who?"

"I noticed three cars outside. I've only seen two of you."

Lawson smiled. "Always on the lookout for trouble, aren't you?"

"It does have a habit of finding me."

"There are six other agents, not including me. They're on the outside of the building maintaining security."

"Expecting someone to crash the party?"

"One never knows, does one?"

"I guess not."

"Relax. If we were planning something against you, we wouldn't have let you in the building with the gun you're carrying."

Recker adjusted his jacket to make sure his gun was still concealed. "So, what's the big secret?"

"It's... complicated."

"So uncomplicate it."

"I can't yet divulge anything until I know you're in."

"In what?"

"The agency," Lawson said. "It's a level five emergency, and the agency wants you back in to complete an assignment."

Recker looked stunned. He stared at her for a minute, not sure if she was yanking his chain or not. Considering most people in the agency didn't have much of a sense of humor, he assumed that was highly doubtful. Recker didn't know what to say. They were words he was sure he would never hear again. If there was anything in this life he was sure of, it was that he'd never work for the CIA again. But it's just like the saying goes, nothing lasts forever.

Lawson could tell he didn't quite know how to respond and wanted to make sure he heard her loud and clear.

"We want you back in."

ABOUT THE AUTHOR

Mike Ryan is a USA Today Bestselling Author. He lives in Pennsylvania with his wife, and four children. He's the author of the bestselling Silencer Series, as well as many others. Visit his website at www.mikeryanbooks.com to find out more about his books, and sign up for his newsletter. You can also interact with Mike via Facebook, and Instagram.

facebook.com/mikeryanauthor
instagram.com/mikeryanauthor

ALSO BY MIKE RYAN

Continue reading The Silencer Series with the next book in the series, Close Range.

Other Books:

The Eliminator Series

The Extractor Series

The Cain Series

The Cari Porter Series

The Ghost Series

The Brandon Hall Series

A Dangerous Man

The Last Job

The Crew

CPSIA information can be obtained
at www.ICGtesting.com
Printed in the USA
LVHW080139160721
692489LV00031B/258/J

9 781953 986139